The Price of Nobility

From the Historian Tales

By Lance Conrad

Praise for The Price of Creation,

first book of The Historian Tales:

"This author deserves to be read..."
> –Tracy Hickman
> *New York Times Bestselling Author*

"Inspiring..."
> –John Forsythe

"Original and refreshing..."
> –Robyn Anderson

"An incredible and enthralling read..."
> –Arianne Clare
> *Bookworm on the Loose (blog)*

"One of the most original stories I have read in years..."
> –Jamie Jensen

"I easily stepped into this world with the Historian as my guide and storyteller..."
> –Carol Stowe

DAWN STAR
PRESS

The following is a work of fiction. All names, places, characters and events portrayed herein are the invention of the author's imagination or are used fictitiously. Any similarity to any real persons or occurrences is purely coincidental.

The Price of Nobility

For information about discounts, bulk purchases, or reproduction of content in this book, please contact Dawn Star Press:

info@dawnstarpress.com

Cover art by Noel Sellon

ISBN: 978-0-9910230-1-1

Printed in the United States of America

For my son,

who gives me hope

Chapter 1

I am the Historian, I am immortal, I am ageless, I am nameless. I am carried by my own feet through times and worlds to witness great stories

This is one such story.

I felt colder than you can possibly imagine.

Somehow the forces that hold death at bay for me welcome the elements with open arms. I have been in situations where I envied people who had frozen to death, as their suffering had an end to it.

I could be frozen to the core, every normal sensation numb from cold, and yet the urge to move on would be as strong as ever.

Lacking a great story, I was cold enough that anything indoors would have been more than enough temptation to hold me for the night. Winter was coming to an end in the land I walked, but the night was cold and the wind was strong.

At that moment, as numbness crept up my arms and legs, I would have settled for a cave or a fallen tree if nothing more hospitable could be found.

To my surprise and delight, a city opened up beneath me over the next hill. In the distance, a broad castle sat over the city like a brooding hen. My luck held and the first building I could see on the outskirts of the city was obviously an inn.

I quickened my pace. I felt like running, but even half-frozen, I still couldn't go scampering off over the country. The dignity of my office, or something like that. I can't honestly say I understand everything I do.

I stepped through the doors into a wall of stuffy warmth and the smell of stale sweat. I moved quickly to the side, hoping the innkeeper wouldn't notice me for a while.

For someone who walks endlessly, money is a pointless burden. One society's valuables are another society's trash, and all of it eventually becomes dead weight.

However, my lifestyle seems to be the polar opposite of innkeepers', who stay in one place their entire life and try to acquire as much of all types of money as possible.

Innkeepers and I have never been able to reconcile this extreme philosophical difference. So most innkeepers simply do not want me around once they discover I have no money, nor any ambitions to acquire any. Some get downright rude about it.

As luck would have it, this innkeeper was quite busy harvesting money from a large group of men. They were all dressed the same and had swords hung at their belts. It didn't take much to see that this was a soldiers' bar.

I successfully worked my way to a corner table that was still hidden in shadow, in spite of the bright fire and several lamps around the room. I slid into the chair, my eyes on the innkeeper. My luck held and his attention was completely focused on the soldiers pressing about the bar.

"Any reason you don't want to be seen?"

I jumped. Not very dignified, being startled like that, but

even a Historian can be surprised. I had been so intent on the innkeeper, I had not noticed that the table in the dark already had two silent occupants. The lights of the room flickered in their eyes as they studied me. The first one spoke again.

"In my experience, people who don't want to be seen are either sneaking up or sneaking away, which are you?"

I smiled sheepishly.

"I am part of a special third group of very cold people; the kind who don't have any money and don't want the innkeeper to ask them to leave before they can enjoy the fire for a while."

The man grunted.

"I suppose it doesn't matter either way, we were about done here. You are welcome to the table and the fire. Everyone else is here for the grog."

The two men had started to retrieve their cloaks from the backs of their chairs when loud voices rang out from the bar. An especially drunk man had lifted his mug above his head, heedless of the pungent ale that sloshed down his arm.

"And this drink, this drink I'm drinking to the health of our dear King Tibian!"

Even in the dim light at the table, I could see my new companions tense as the drunkard continued his toast.

"May he live long, or at least long enough for someone to drag him down from his pillows and wine and bleed him like he has bled us!"

Several voices cheered loudly, but most of the men had gone quiet. I knew nothing of the political situation in this land, but to hear a soldier talking about his king that way could easily be taken as treason. The fact that so many had still cheered told

3

me that things were not all right in this kingdom.

The man I had been talking to rose and moved around the table like a cat stalking its prey. His eyes were fixed on the drunk man who was now doing his best to keep his feet beneath him as he drank even more.

The men surrounding the drunk fell silent and moved away as the man from the table approached. They had been cheering right along, nearly as drunk as their friend, but they sobered quickly under the fiery glare of my new acquaintance. The drunk saw him as he approached and began a feeble explanation.

"Now, Captain, all I..."

The drunkard's attempt at justification gurgled to a halt as the Captain's hand snaked out, the web of his hand striking the man's throat. A harder blow could have killed the man. I was certain the restraint was intentional.

As it was, the man fell to his knees, suddenly sober as he grabbed at his throat and gasped for wisps of air through his bruised windpipe. His eyes were pleading as he looked up at his Captain, expecting a finishing blow.

None came. Instead the Captain's gaze fell on each of the men around him in turn. Each looked down or away under the intensity of his stare. The room had fallen completely silent; so when he spoke, barely above a whisper, he could be heard clearly throughout the room.

"Guard your tongues, men. I will not stand for such a gross breach of discipline from any under my command. Is that clear?"

No response was expected. None came.

4

"Innkeeper, the bar is closed for the rest of the night. The men will return to their barracks."

I leaned forward. They called him Captain, but the man spoke with all the authority of a general. Every last man in the inn moved to obey, even those who weren't soldiers. Such authority did not come from position. This was a man of personal power.

Men shuffled out of the inn, avoiding eye contact with anyone else. The Captain walked back to the table, his stride unchanged by the tide of men around him. They flowed around him like a river around a boulder. He turned to me as the two of them finished putting on their cloaks.

"Well, stranger, I'm afraid I have cost you your fire. I am truly sorry about that. I hate to see a man put out in the cold if he has nowhere to go. If you don't mind a bit of a walk, you can come with us."

I have never minded a walk.

Chapter 2

All feel justified. To find truth, a man must consider the possibility that he is wrong.

-Musings of the Historian

"So then, traveler, what should we call you?"

"Call me whatever you wish," I responded. I immediately regretted my quick response as the Captain glanced over at me, suspicion and irritation in his eyes.

"You moved into that inn like you were trying to avoid someone. Now you won't tell me your name? You don't strike me as a criminal or a spy, but you aren't giving me much reason to trust you. Perhaps we should be taking a walk to the blockhouse instead of a warm hearth."

"You see..." My mind raced through possible explanations. Each one died on my lips as I met his eyes.

They were a pale blue and focused like lightning. This was not a man I could lie to. He saw too much and thought too deeply. In the end, after stammering for a moment, I decided to try the truth, some of it, anyway.

"You see, the fact is, I don't actually know my name. People have usually given me a name wherever I went and that suits me fine."

The Captain scowled at this, searching my face for any kind of deception. The hard lines in his face softened a little as a trace of pity entered his eyes. The suspicion remained, but it was tempered with the thought that perhaps I was in greater need than he had known.

"What do you remember of your younger days? Did you have a family? Were you abandoned?"

I shook my head.

"I cannot say with any surety. I remember nothing of my childhood. Still, I do not believe that I was abandoned. Sometimes, when I dream, I feel the love and warmth of family. I think I must have known it once."

This was only partly a lie. I never actually slept, so I never actually dreamed. However, when out wandering, when time got fuzzy and the horizons shifted, I would get the faintest glimmers of lost emotions and memories. They were never anything I could piece together into a full image, just scraps.

"I have known men who became addled after a strong blow to the head or having too much to drink, but they all recovered their wits and their memories after a good night's sleep. Have you really lost so much of your life?"

"Not remembering it, I have no idea what I have lost." I smiled. "I have been wandering for as long as I can remember, I have no other life to compare it to but what I see in my travels."

"How does a man live without a name?" It was the younger man who spoke now for the first time. I looked to him, trying to study out his features by moonlight.

He was several years younger than the other man, but only slightly shorter. His face held confusion and suspicion, but they were clearly not natural emotions for him. His face was built for smiling, though he was making a direct effort to look as serious as his companion.

Past these simple observations, one thing became clear: these men were brothers. I hadn't noticed the family resemblance during the confusion at the inn. When he spoke, however, the voices were practically identical. They also had the same shape of face and brow, though the older one had darker hair, almost black.

The younger one had seemed content to let his older brother handle the situation up to this point. Apparently, he could keep quiet no longer. He pressed his question.

"I mean, a man lives to bring honor to his name, to his family. What do you do if you don't even have a name to bring honor to?"

His older brother, the Captain, gave him a withering look. The younger man melted under the scorching gaze, suddenly realizing how rude his question had been.

"I'm sorry, I just meant..." He stammered. I spoke quickly to rescue him.

"It's fine, I have often asked myself the same question. All men have different roles. Surely a farmer or a blacksmith could argue that their role in society is more vital than another.

"Each would be right in their own way. The blacksmith would starve without the farmer's produce; and the farmer's land would be much harder to work without the tools the blacksmith makes.

"When all is said and done, each man has to use the gifts he's been given. We would waste our lives if we only looked to what we don't have.

"As for me, my role is an observer, a storyteller. After all, what use is a smith's blade, a farmer's fresh bread, or a soldier's quiet sacrifice, if none remember it? That is my role. I see what men do with the time they are given. I remember them."

"Do you judge them, traveler?" It was the Captain who spoke now. His voice was as intense as ever, but out of nowhere there was a tone of desperation. The man who commanded with such confidence suddenly seemed unsure of himself. I was equally unsure how to respond.

Something I had said had struck a deep chord in the quiet military man.

"Umm, I suppose that would depend on how you see judgment." I stalled. "The limitations of time force me to judge who and what I should stay around to witness.

"However, I don't believe any man can know the end from the beginning. Only a man himself knows what is in his heart."

It was a cliché bit of fluff. The captain waved it away with irritation. He had been walking slightly ahead of our group as we travelled through the night, leading the party. He rounded on me, stopping our little party just outside the city.

His face, barely visible under a waning moon, was deadly serious. He locked onto my eyes and I knew that he would know any lie I attempted. I resolved to tell the truth and see where it led. The questions came rapid fire.

"Are you from this land?"

"No."

"Do you know anything about us or our people?"

"No."

"Have you seen other lands, other peoples?"

"Many."

"Have you seen good men?"

"Few."

"Have you seen evil men?"

"More."

"Do you believe that man has a soul?"

"I know it."

"Would you always tell me the truth?"

"No."

This last answer brought him up short. I still don't know what he wanted from me, but it was important to him. I had seen men before who looked like the Captain did at that moment.

It was the look of a man trapped, forced into a corner and facing defeat. Such men were capable of terrible things. What the Captain wanted, I didn't know, but I knew he wanted it more than anything.

"Are you saying you would lie to me?" He continued after pausing for a moment to absorb my last response.

"Now then, if I were going to lie to you, that would have been a good time to do it, wouldn't it? I simply meant that not all truths are yours. I will not answer a question you have no right to ask of me. Some truths are mine alone."

He paused again, his eyes searching mine. Finally he nodded, more to himself than to me. Something had satisfied him and his confident manner fell back around him like a cloak.

"I can respect that, traveler. I would like you to come with us. I will tell you up front that I would like you to learn of us and my people. Once you have done so to your satisfaction, I want you to judge me."

"Simeon! You can't...!" His younger brother protested, the

Captain raised a hand to silence him.

"Even criminals feel they are justified in their actions. How can we be so sure of ourselves?"

"But you can't..." The brother grasped for words, trying to voice some valid argument. "There is too much at stake!"

The Captain nodded.

"That is exactly why we must question ourselves, Joseph. However, if it will ease your mind, if at any time this traveler seems like he will betray us, you may kill him yourself. Would that pacify you?"

The younger man's face paled, but he nodded weakly. The Captain then turned to me.

"You must understand right now what you would be getting into. As Joseph has already made clear, we face a matter of life and death. Honestly, my reasons for including you are purely selfish.

"If you would like out of this, say so now and we will speak no more of it. I will see to it that you are back on your way warm and fed. Perhaps I could even get you to tell me a story or two before you go.

"But if you agree to come with us, it must be a complete commitment. Once you have heard our story, I must insist that you remain with us until the end. What do you say?"

I am not ashamed to say I felt downright giddy. Any historian who would pass up such an intrigue was no historian at all. I kept my emotions reined in and nodded solemnly, as befitted the situation.

"I will make my place with yours until your story is done. I hope you will appreciate that I cannot offer judgment until I feel that the story has played out completely."

"Of course."

We shook hands in the old style, clasping forearms, to seal the deal. The rest of the walk passed in silence, each man lost in his own musings, until we came upon our destination.

Chapter 3

*To weaken the body, remove blood. To weaken the
character, remove struggle.*
                              −Musings of the Historian

It took another twenty minutes of walking to reach our
destination. I guess the brothers enjoyed their solitude. Their
dwelling was a squat, solid stone block of a house. The
craftsmanship was quite good, though built for defense more than
appearance.

"Our father built it." The Captain answered my unspoken
question. "Back when he was a young man, Marauders from the
East would raid through this land. Some men would fight, some
would run, some would win, and some would lose.

"In the end, so much was destroyed in the melee it didn't
matter much whether they won or lost. Their homes were ravaged
one way or another. My father built stone walls on top of his log
home, working with his sword lying next to his tools.

"When he was attacked, he would stand and fight. In the
end, I think the Marauders came to fear his sword more than his
strong walls. In any event, by the time the house was done, few
ever attacked.

"Shortly after, King Stephan brought the clan chiefs
together in alliance and formed the Land Guard, a force large
enough and strong enough to secure the territory against the

Marauders.

"Our father served with the Guard for years, so the stone house went unused until the war was over. He finally retired and came home to find a wife to bear him sons. Two sons."

By then we were settled inside the dark structure, and Joseph set to work building a fire. He had skilled hands and the fire sprang to life in no time, lighting the solid structure to the corners. It spoke of military men. Everything was in its place, no space was wasted or decorated.

If one looked carefully, one could see edges and handles of various weapons placed around the room, where they would be at hand if something unexpected happened.

I noticed that Joseph never strayed far from one handle or another, always keeping an eye on me. Simeon, however, lounged at ease, having already mentally included me in their plans.

Joseph busied himself around the house and soon I had a piece of bread and a bowl of soup in my hands. Warm food and a warm fire had been all I had wanted less than an hour earlier. Now it was the story that held my attention.

So far, it was the same story I had heard thousands of times. It was the way kingdoms were born out of chaos, order from madness. He didn't make me wait long.

"King Stephan was a good king, and he conquered when he was still young. He was as good at peace as he was at war, and the kingdom flourished. Our borders grew ever more secure. As our people felt safe, they spread out, they traded, and they loved their king.

"It seems to me that people started to think that Stephan would be their king forever. But even kings are mortal."

14

Simeon was a natural storyteller, and he felt strongly about the subject. He paused, a sadness in his eyes, I worried that I was going to lose him to reverie.

"What happened?" I nudged.

"A plague." He answered simply. "A devastating plague hit our kingdom. It seemed to be random in its selection, but where it touched, none survived. Nothing could cool the fever. Nothing could dull the pain of the suffering.

"We lost our father, we lost our mother, and we lost our King. It was the winter the world ended, or at least it felt like it. Perhaps worst of all, it also destroyed the royal family. The crown prince perished, as did the Queen and all of the children, save the youngest son."

"Tibian?" I guessed, remembering who the drunk had been toasting at the bar. Simeon nodded.

"Yes, young Tibian, who was only a boy at the time. For years, the kingdom was run by advisers. They manipulated the boy and fought over him for their own advancement and agendas.

"The Land Guard became fractured, torn by infighting. Luckily for us, the Marauders in the East were as decimated by the plague as we were, so there were none to take advantage of our weakness.

"Finally, the boy king came of age and wrested the throne back from his advisers. The Land Guard supported him in this, uniting at last in a common cause. All hoped for better times, a return of Stephan."

"I take it the boy was no Stephan." I guessed. The story was hitting all of the stereotypes. The boy king would have been flattered and pampered endlessly by the sycophantic counselors.

Such luxuries are ruinous to a young character. Simeon shook his head sadly.

"The palace intrigues and power struggles were over, the King was on his throne. However, it soon became clear how simple his rule would be."

The Captain paused now. He knew he was crossing the point of no return. What he would say next would be treason, likely far worse than what he had punished back at the inn. He may have hesitated for my benefit. After all, charges of treason were seldom selective.

Just by hearing this, I would be implicating myself, endangering my own life over words I had heard. After a moment's reflection, his eyes steeled and he pressed on.

"He taxes the people harshly. Those in his inner circle live a life of luxury far beyond what Stephan would have ever allowed. The rest of the people are ignored.

"Things carried on for a while under their own momentum, but the drag of taxes eventually took its toll. Business slowed, crops were left in the field because farmers knew that to harvest them meant to turn them over to the crown.

"That was ten years ago. Things have gone from bad to worse. The Land Guard is now just a collection of different factions. We fight each other almost as often as the Marauders, though that isn't hard.

"You see, the raids have all but stopped. The attacks that come now have a different feel to them. They are becoming ordered in their attacks, probing and retreating. I think they are testing us.

"There are whispers of a new king in the East, someone

who is uniting the Marauders and training them into an army. If this is true, our kingdom is all but lost.

"The Land Guard could never put up a true defense at this point. Most of the commanders don't even know each other; some don't even know their own men."

"So something must be done." I finished for him. He nodded in agreement and the conversation was over. My eyes wandered to the door, considering the open road beyond.

This was a story I had seen before, far too many times. A young military leader makes a grab for power from a despotic king.

Sometimes it worked, sometimes it didn't. Sometimes the new king was an improvement, more often he wasn't. I liked the Captain, but it seemed to me that the rest of this story would just be bloodshed. And boring.

Still, I had told him that I would remain with him. Maybe I could witness one more coup. I hoped a more interesting story wasn't happening just over the horizon, maybe with this new king of the Marauders.

I laid down on the worn cot they offered me and waited until morning. It was a long night. Before sunrise, I heard them get quietly out of bed and get dressed. I remained motionless, "sleeping." I had found that the best way to avoid suspicion was to not do anything suspicious.

Travelers who finally get a place to rest sleep until something wakes them up. Neither of them had been loud enough yet to give me an excuse to say I had woken up.

In fact, I was quite impressed by their stealth as I realized they had also managed to strap on some hardened leather armor and wrist bands. I also caught a glimpse of some strange looking swords.

I waited until I heard a series of dulls thwacks before I rolled out of bed to have a peek outside at what they were doing.

The two men stood apart from each other in the clearing, strange brown blades flicking back and forth in furious attacks and parries. I tried to get a closer look at the swords, but it was too far and they were moving too fast to get a clear look.

I am an ardent fan of sword fighting.

In my travels I have seen a great many fighters. The weapons have ranged from sticks and stones to reciprocating sonic pulsers. Where there is a weapon, there is a master of that weapon. Any time you get to see a master use his weapon, it is art.

Never is this truer than with a sword. I have seen swordsmen who seemed to dance through the air, the sword an extension of their own body.

They seemed to be completely alone, lost in their dance, as their enemies fell around them, as if in reverence. But that is another story.

Both brothers had skill, though I would have hesitated to call them masters. It was the kind of sword fighting taught to soldiers, used in groups and tight quarters. It was simple, direct, and deadly.

There was no doubt in my mind that there were none in the Land Guard that could have matched them. Of course, I also doubted that any of the Land Guard were up before the sun to train as hard as these two.

They were tireless. The swords clacked back and forth in a steady rhythm as one pressed the attack, then the other. Their breath was white and wispy in the frozen morning air and it puffed steadily above them as if they were two steam engines.

Every now and then, Joseph's blade would twitch a bit too far in response to some feint or counterattack from Simeon and the Captain would score a hit on his younger brother, tapping his leather jerkin or arms.

In many training sessions I've watched, a solid hit such as that would have meant a break in the action before a new round began, or perhaps a chance to go over what had happened and advice on how to do better.

That was not the case with these two. Nothing changed at all when Simeon would score a hit. Joseph would nod slightly, then press forward into another attempt to break past the elder's wall-like defense.

It made a lot of sense. The last thing you would ever want to teach a soldier is that he should stop when struck. If anything, he should act more decisively than ever to save his life. A pause at the moment of impact would be fatal, giving your opponent another fraction of a second to finish you off.

Whatever the blades were, they weren't metal. There was no clang when the blades met, and there was no blood drawn when blade met flesh.

The only sign of humanity from either of them was when one sizzling fast attack landed right across Joseph's knuckles and he yelped. To his credit, he did not drop his sword and even managed to sidestep a follow up thrust.

It occurred to me I had been given my opening. That yelp was plenty loud enough to awaken a sleeping traveler, assuming he slept light. The sun had also risen while the two men were training.

While it didn't seem to give off any warmth, it did send rays of light into the small stone house. It was time for me to make my appearance.

"Is everyone all right?" I called out from the open door, doing my best to look sleepy. Simeon's eyes flicked towards me for just a moment, long enough for Joseph to slip his sword point past his brother's guard and land a light tap on the leather chest plate.

Joseph danced away, a broad smile on his face. Simeon threw him an annoyed scowl, then turned to walk over to me.

"Yes, traveler, everyone is fine. My brother hurt his poor little fingers."

Now it was Joseph's turn to scowl at his brother's retreating back. As Simeon drew closer, I could see the sweat coursing down his face. For the ease with which they moved, the two brothers had been working very hard.

I could see the swords now up close. They were made from some kind of heavy wood. Raw leather had been wrapped and stitched around the blade, wetted, and allowed to dry. As the leather dried, it shrank and hardened, compressing the wood and making it very hard to crack.

It was impossible to tell what other modifications may have been made without a closer inspection, but these practice swords were close to the real thing in balance and weight, more than sufficient to give the men a good training without hurting each other.

At least not too bad, I amended my thought, as they moved closer to me. I could see that the hardened leather had dark stains on it that could only be blood.

20

Simeon noticed my interest in the sword and misunderstood. He offered me the weapon, handle first.

"If you would like to train for a little bit, it is a good way to get the blood flowing on a cold morning like this. I'm sure Joseph would be happy to spar with you."

I raised my hands in a warding gesture, shaking my head and smiling.

"I was more interested in how it was put together. I wouldn't know the first thing about using a sword. I feel that I am too old now to start learning."

"A man is never too old to learn something new, and the time may come when you might need it." Simeon insisted, proffering me the practice sword one more time. I shook my head again.

"I'm afraid I can't. A soldier might sometimes be a storyteller, but a storyteller cannot sometimes be a soldier. If I am to judge your story, I cannot be preparing myself to be a part of it."

Simeon puzzled over my words for a moment, then shrugged and leaned the sword against the house.

"I suppose we all have our roles to play in what is about to happen. I promise to do what I can to protect you should danger arise, but I hope you'll forgive me if one day I find my priorities divided."

"Of course I understand. If you ever had to choose between your brother and a stranger, none would question your choice. However, now that you bring it up, what does happen next?"

Simeon nodded, unsurprised at my question. What was

surprising was how fast Joseph snuck forward to listen.

It struck me that Joseph didn't know any better than I did what his brother had planned. His loyalty had made his stand clear before he even heard the call to battle.

So we two sat in silence, waiting to hear what Simeon would say of his planned future. In a frustrating show of nonchalance, Simeon had turned his attention to removing his training armor and rummaging about for a simple breakfast of bread and cheese.

I looked to Joseph, but he only shrugged. He would wait on his brother, trusting to his wisdom. He didn't trust me enough to side with me in pressing for information. So it came down to me. I simply had to get him talking and the rest would become clear.

I had seen plenty of military takeovers and the format was fairly straightforward. First, an ambitious man, for reasons that seemed good to him, would gather supporters around him.

This not only served to increase his strength and chances for success, but would also cement in his own mind the righteousness of his cause.

Then came a tipping point. By the time a man had enough supporters to make the coup happen, it was already too late for him to turn back, even if he wanted to.

Since it was obvious that Simeon was ready to move, his supporter base must be broad and powerful. He was no fool, after all. Therefore, this seemed like the perfect place to get the conversation moving.

"Will the others be joining us soon?" I probed. This close to a takeover, there must be daily meetings, at least among the key commanders.

Simeon, however, looked confused, and maybe a little angry.

"What others? If you know of someone else who knows of this and haven't told me about it, you will regret it, I promise you."

"No, no, no." I hurried to reassure him. "I simply meant the others who will be helping you. Surely you don't mean to move the world with only you and your brother."

I meant the last bit simply as a bit of a joke to diffuse the tension in the room. Still, Simeon looked fondly at his brother and mused softly.

"I suppose we could try, traveler." He spoke to me, though he looked to his brother. "You'd be a fool to bet against us, in any event. However, I have thought a long time about this and I do believe we will need another."

Joseph leaned closer, interested, as I leaned back, flabbergasted. I still trusted my instincts about people and could not believe that Simeon was stupid or insane. Still, he seemed to be talking about taking the throne with three men.

At least, I assumed the third person would be a man, perhaps it was a woman. It seemed I was taking too much for granted recently. For all I knew, the third member was a spirit, or a dog, or a fish. The possibilities were endless when you abandoned common sense.

He had made it clear that his sights were set no lower than the throne, but to try and take it with three men would be suicide.

Even if some miracle of strategy and luck occurred to place him in the chair, it would only last as long as it took for someone with ten men to decide he wanted a turn at being king and threw Simeon off.

I shook my head slightly, symbolically banishing my preconceived notions from my head. It was time for me to admit that I didn't actually know what was going on. Simeon hadn't said anything more and didn't seem like he was going to, but he had managed to capture my attention once again.

With one more look out the window to the distant horizon, I bid it a temporary farewell in my heart and turned myself back into the stone cottage, intent on seeing this story through to its end.

I didn't have long to wait for my next chapter, only the space of one more meal. When Simeon finished his breakfast, he stood.

"Well, no reason to wait, let's go see if he'll join us!"

Chapter 4

There is a stark honesty in desperation.

–Musings of the Historian

If you took a scoop of earth and placed it in a jar of water, shook it, then left it to sit, it would promptly stop being a scoop of earth. Some bits would float to the top, taking advantage of the situation to put some distance between them and their fellows.

Some parts would dissolve into the water, losing themselves entirely.

And some parts would shoot right to the bottom, waiting there until they were surrounded by other drifting sediment that they could push around.

So it is with human beings when the society they are used to falls apart and everything is shaken up. Criminals, hard and rough like little pieces of gravel, push around those they see as sediment until running into a bigger piece of gravel.

The neighborhood we were walking into was all too familiar. When a land suffered, slums formed like mold. They spread out like rancid spiderwebs, waiting to trap the fallen.

It was a place where human life would be cheap, discarded over petty arguments or shiny trinkets.

Both my companions knew they were being watched, though neither gave any sign of it. They walked confidently, showing no sign of weakness.

In spite of the lingering cold, their cloaks were pulled back to display their swords, hanging loose and ready at their waists.

Whenever we were reasonably alone, Joseph and I would take turns pelting Simeon with questions.

"Who is it we are going to see?" I asked.

"The only man who can pull off what we need done."

"What sort of man could you find in a place like this?"

"A man who wants to be left alone by people like us."

That didn't sound promising at all. At the next open place, Joseph picked up where I had left off.

"But the only person I can think of who's down here would be..."

Simeon nodded. Joseph's confident stride faltered. His hand strayed to the handle of his sword and his eyes began darting around.

"Is it true what they say about him?"

Simeon smiled.

"I suspect that the rumors don't capture half of it. I have heard stories that would put the gossips' tales to shame."

"Where did you hear these stories?"

"From Father. He witnessed most of them with his own eyes."

"Father knew him?" Joseph was incredulous. "Why haven't I heard of this before now?"

"Father told me about him only a couple months before the plague took him. You were still a bit young for such stories. Looking back on it, I think I was a bit young for such stories, to tell the truth.

26

"I wonder now if Father had some idea that he wouldn't be around much longer. I think he wanted me to know who could help us if things got really bad. I figure things are pretty bad now."

"Why would he help us?"

"Who are we talking about?!" I interrupted, almost shouting, my curiosity finally breaking past my manners. Simeon and Joseph turned back to me as if seeing me for the first time.

"Oh yes, I forgot that you aren't from around here, though you must have traveled far not to know of this man. Even the Marauders have their own name for him.

"He was a young man when our father was in the Land Guard. Even then, Father said he was the deadliest warrior anyone had ever seen. He could move right through the middle of a Marauder camp undetected.

"There was no wall he couldn't climb, nor any weapon he couldn't wield. He chafed under military order and went rogue, waging his own personal war against the Marauders.

"He took the fight to them in their camps and strongholds. The stories that came back were the stuff of nightmares.

"When the war was over, the King granted him a pardon for his desertion, since he had still fought the enemy bravely. Frankly, most believe that Stephan pardoned him because there were none who dared to arrest him.

"After the war, he faded away and no one heard any more from him. After the plague, he showed up here in the slums.

"His name is Asher. Around here he is a court of final justice. If someone has truly been wronged, they can come to him and ask for his help, for a price. The stories say that if he believes you, your enemies die. If he doesn't believe you, you die. Either way, he keeps the money."

"So what if he doesn't believe us?"

The question hung in the air unanswered. We all took a moment to digest this before Joseph returned to his first interrupted question.

"So why would he help us?"

"Father said that Asher owed him a debt, one he would remember. He didn't tell me what it was, but I have bet our lives on him being right about that."

He explained it matter-of-factly. There was no offer of backing out. He knew I couldn't and he knew his brother wouldn't. All that remained now was to roll the dice.

He finally led us to a seedy looking inn right on the river. The stench of stale ale and old sewage hung ripe in the air.

Why anyone who had a choice would choose to live in such a place was well beyond me. I had seen trash heaps that were cleaner.

The men inside the inn already knew we were coming. Their knives and swords were all bared and set on the tables in front of them. While not overtly threatening, the implication was clear: the Guard had no business being here.

Simeon ignored them and went straight to the bartender, an obscenely fat man who glowered at them over heavy jowls.

"We're looking for Asher."

The bartender's mouth curled up in a wicked smile. He nodded toward a door leading to a back room.

"Wonderful! Asher lets me keep the clothes and weapons. Good luck."

He chuckled to himself, making the sweaty rolls on his neck jiggle. We left him cackling and headed into the room, Simeon in the lead, I to his left and Joseph on the right.

I closed the door behind us. Joseph gripped his sword handle openly, his eyes fixed on the sight before him.

The room was empty except for a solid oak table with a chair behind it, facing the door. A figure sat motionless at the chair, cold and ominous. A fire raged in the fireplace directly behind him.

The light from the fire lit everything around the man, casting him in a dark silhouette. In spite of the oppressive heat, the man wore a heavy cloak with a large hood that pulled his face even deeper into the shadows.

The hood twitched slightly, an acknowledgment of our entrance, but nothing more. He said nothing, waiting for one of us to speak. Even bold Simeon was momentarily at a loss for words. The room sat in silence for several heavy seconds.

It was Joseph who broke the moment, leaning forward to place a bag of gold coins on the table in front of the seated man. He had no idea how such things were done, but figured he should make their intentions clear before something bad happened.

The motion stirred Simeon out of his stupor. He spoke with a confidence he clearly didn't feel.

"Asher, my name is Simeon. I am the son of Ander, he claimed you owed him a debt."

Simeon fell silent a moment, hoping he hadn't crossed a line. Or perhaps he hoped that the name would spark something in the sinister figure, something to make him seem more human.

As it was, the hooded man gave no sign of recognition, no

further sound or movement. He may as well have been one of the shadows he seemed to command. Simeon finally cleared his throat and continued.

"We need your help. If you feel any debt towards my family, you can clear it now." Simeon's voice grew stronger as he warmed to the task.

"And if you still feel any sort of duty or loyalty to this land, I ask you to help me save it. You are the only one who can help me make a difference here."

He stopped again. Surely Asher would need to respond now, some sort of affirmation. Joseph's knuckles were white on the hilt of his sword. I wasn't sure if he even knew he was gripping it. Still the seconds dragged on in silence.

"Why does the son of Ander need someone to do his killing for him?"

Any courage our little band had mustered melted away in an instant. Even I, who couldn't die, felt my knees gel and my stomach clench.

The voice, low, dark and deadly, had come from directly behind us.

Simeon turned slowly, his hands raising in a peaceful gesture. My mind went to the stories. If he had considered a supplicant unworthy, they would have been dead before they felt the knife. I had no doubt that he could have killed all three of us before we had any time to react.

He directed his next statement to the man at the table.

"Bartus, I have no more need of your services this afternoon, you may go."

The intimidating figure at the table reached up and

pushed back the hood. To my surprise, it was an old man. He had scars around his mouth and his jaw sat at an odd angle, as if he had been chewing something particularly tough and his face had frozen mid-chew.

He nodded to Asher, then limped back to the corner of the room and disappeared through a door I hadn't noticed before. It was so well crafted that it blended seamlessly into the wall. I wondered what craftsman had been convinced to do such fine work on such a decrepit building.

Asher moved around the table and sat down at the newly vacant chair. The fire still hid many of his features, but what we could see was enough to know that this was a force to be reckoned with.

His hair was jet black, with a few wisps of gray that only served to make the rest seem that much blacker. It was cut short, hacked away by some blade obviously not meant for that purpose.

His features were sharp and harsh, his eyes as black as his hair. His arms, corded with muscle and marked with angry scars, rested before him on the table.

The flickering light from the fire lit up his face enough to know he was scowling at each of us in turn. His gaze finally rested on Simeon.

"I don't tend to talk much in these little meetings; or at all, for that matter. So I hope you appreciate the fact that I don't like to repeat myself.

"I ask you again, why does a son of Ander need help with a killing? Is it the blood that unsettles you, boy?"

The taunt stung Simeon visibly, but he squared his shoulders to Asher as he replied.

"You know what is happening out there. You see how these people suffer. You also know what will happen when the Marauders return. We need to do something about the king."

Asher's face turned slightly upward in an expression that couldn't quite be called a smile.

"At least the son of Ander isn't a coward, you've aimed your sights high enough, boy. However, it is still sad to see that Ander sired a fool. And you are a fool if you believe that assassinating the king would do anything at all to help.

"If I believed that, I would have had his skull as my soup bowl many years ago. Surely you are not so blind to think that the death of the king would lead to anything but civil war."

I was only a passive observer, but I was glad that this scary man had raised the points that he did. They were the same problems I had myself, though I didn't feel that I was the man to voice them.

Perhaps Asher would let the brothers leave without killing them, and even dissuade them from their plan of rebellion. Simeon, however, surprised us all.

"I had no intention of asking you to kill King Tibian. I want you to take him."

For that moment in time, Simeon was the one in control as Asher tried to understand.

"I don't quite follow you, boy."

"No? If you think it through, you'll see the logic is quite inevitable. The country needs a strong king and a good king. The king we have is neither."

"No arguments so far."

"Trying to replace him will only result in bloodshed and

more weakness in the kingdom, which we can't afford."

"Yes, yes, which is why we can do nothing." Asher's voice betrayed the frustration he felt at the hopeless situation.

"No. That is why we must take the king we have and make him strong, and good."

Asher leaned forward, as if seeing Simeon for the first time, his eyes searching.

"So not a coward, and not a fool. But perhaps out of your mind. What makes you think you could make that spoiled brat into anything else?"

"Who made him spoiled? Who ruined him? Was it not the spoiled and ruined excuses for men who were in his service?

"Who made us men? Who made us strong? Was it not our fathers and brothers who showed us what it meant to be strong?

"Our experiences made us who we are, just as his experiences molded him. It is time he had experiences that taught him what our fathers taught us: how to be a man."

Asher spoke softly, almost to himself.

"Not a coward, not a fool, and not a boy. Have you considered what this means for you? What it means for those you include?"

Simeon nodded and Asher continued.

"Have they?"

I nodded, a mirror of Joseph who nodded on the other side. I didn't know if Joseph truly had, but I did know he would never leave Simeon.

"This one is obviously your brother, another son of Ander. Who is this?" A scarred hand gestured towards me.

"A stranger." Simeon replied simply. Asher raised a

curious eyebrow.

"You trust him?"

"Absolutely."

Silence fell in the room for another ponderous pause before Asher broke it.

"I will take him in one week, where would you like him delivered?"

I was stunned. He may as well have been delivering flowers. There was no further question of plans, resources, or strategy. He simply stated what he could do and none doubted it.

"Go to my father's house and head north about five miles. We will have things prepared and leave from there."

Asher nodded. I noted that he did not ask where the two brothers lived.

"You may go, the men outside won't bother you if they know you have my approval."

"How will they know we have your approval?" Joseph spoke for the first time. Asher looked surprised at the question.

"Because you're not dead, of course."

Chapter 5

The easiest way to be invisible is to stand where no one is looking.

—Musings of the Historian

My head was brimming with questions for Simeon as we left the inn. The men around us now gave curt nods of respect as they saw us leaving. Even the bartender gave an apologetic shrug as we walked by.

Still, I knew that this would be a bad time and place for us to discuss the implications of kidnapping a king.

I managed to hold my tongue until we were traveling across a large field, with no one in sight as far as the eye could see. Then it all came out at once. I felt like a little kid in a classroom.

"When did you decide to kidnap the king? What are you planning to do to change him? Are there others who are going to help in this? Don't you realize you will be executed even if your plan somehow works...?"

And so on. Simeon watched me until my torrent of questions had run out.

"Honestly, traveler, I can't even remember all of those questions to answer them. However, to all of them, I say, 'wait and see.'"

The next week was spent gathering materials. Try as I

might, I couldn't quite seem to string them together into any sort of pattern. We quietly gathered rope, shovels, blocks of wood, a pick, more practice swords, some sugared candy, and a shaving razor.

Simeon spent a lot of time picking out the blocks of wood, poring over their features as if he could see the future written in their grains.

It was near the end of the week when he finally seemed satisfied with the five blocks he had acquired. Last minute preparations filled the time until the day came for the promised delivery.

Obviously, it was too much for me to sit and wait. I would have to get closer to the action.

When a person does one thing over and over again, he or she will become better and better at whatever it is they are doing.

This is how masters are created, by dedicated practice, a prolonged focus on a single activity. Natural talent can speed up the process, but nothing will ever replace the raw power of repetition.

Let me point out a relevant example. In my peculiar life I have various gifts that I was granted by whatever powers may be. For instance, you may have noticed from my stories that I inspire trust in people quite easily.

This is invaluable in collecting my stories. However, I have never gotten any better at it, because it isn't a skill, just a gift.

Here is my skill: I walk. I walk more than any other person has in all the history of all the worlds. I have walked more miles than any bird has ever flown, more than any fish has ever swam.

I have spent more time walking than I have in all other pursuits combined, and many times over, at that. I have walked laps around empty worlds over every terrain seen by man and several that will only ever be witnessed by my eyes.

Therefore, I feel it is safe to say that I may be the most accomplished walker ever to... well, walk.

Some may find this a rather useless skill, but many skills appear that way until they are raised to a high level of mastery.

So what can a master walker do? I can walk faster than many men can run. I can walk without ever tiring. I can walk comfortably up slopes that only insects and lizards would attempt. I can walk through water, mud, or deep sand and it will scarcely subtract a beat from my gait.

Most importantly for this story, I can walk without making a sound, and I can walk without being seen. One might think that someone with sufficient alertness or skill in searching the shadows would find me out, but the law of practice will not be denied. Their skills at searching will never match my endless lifetimes of walking.

So it was that I found myself following Asher as he left his hovel on the appointed evening. I had made my excuses to the brothers, though they didn't seem to care one way or the other.

Their minds were solidly on the task before them. I slipped quickly down to the slums so I wouldn't miss seeing Asher at work.

I knew that he would deliver on his promise of capturing the king. I desperately wanted to see how he would pull it off. I was a little worried that he would take him by sheer force, ripping down all in his path.

Even though the palace was full of guards and army patrols ringed the city, I couldn't quite imagine a scenario in which Asher wouldn't come out the master.

There was death about the man, a quiet lethality usually reserved for the most venomous serpents.

Though I had witnessed endless battles and bloodbaths, I still was not hardened to them and the thought of seeing one that night left my stomach feeling quite unsettled.

So it was with great relief that I followed Asher away from the lights of the main entrances and towards the lonely pools of darkness that gathered around the bases of the towers.

I stilled myself and strained every sense to see better what he was doing. He was dressed all in black, as one might expect, with a deep cowl worn over his head.

Once at the wall, he lowered his hood so he could peer up at the wall before him. I had hoped to see his face, but as soon as he lowered the hood I could see that he had painted himself black. If anything, he sank deeper into the darkness.

He seemed to be fiddling with his sleeves, though I couldn't see why. I was as close as I dared go. Finally, his preparations finished, he sprung at the wall and clung to it like a lizard. I heard a faint scratching noise like metal on stone and then he was climbing.

The sheer stone wall may as well have been a ladder for how easily Asher climbed, moving from one hold to the next effortlessly. If I didn't know better, I would think he had made this climb many times before.

The thought brought me up short. Perhaps I didn't know better after all. Asher had mentioned in passing that he had contemplated killing the king himself. Maybe a man like Asher liked to make such contemplations within striking distance.

It was a chilling thought that a man like Asher may have stood over the king's bed multiple times before this, calmly weighing the pros and cons of murdering him in his sleep.

He slipped through what I assumed was the king's window and I was once again left alone in the dark. I didn't have to wait long, though, because after a short few minutes, Asher's shadowy form once again lifted itself onto the wall and started working its way down to the ground.

I was surprised to see him descending alone, but immediately felt sheepish for thinking so. Even a climber as accomplished as Asher would have had no chance of descending a sheer wall with the weight of another person to drag them down.

I realized that I had become a little caught up in Asher's almost superhuman abilities. I imagine his enemies also had occasion to imagine him doing impossible things. The man was like fear itself, insidious and unreasonable.

He reached the ground easily and moved quickly to his left, where he rummaged around for a while on the ground. I couldn't see what he was doing, but it appeared he was changing clothes and doing something new to his face.

When he finally straightened, he didn't do so fully, rather he came up in a hunch, like a cripple or an old man. When he set out, he didn't do so with his usual walk, full of death and confidence. Instead, he shuffled, dragging one foot behind him, completing the image of an old beggar.

When he rounded the corner of the castle and once again

stood in the light, I could see that the black was gone from his face. Instead he looked old and dirty, worn down by long years and hard labor.

His sleek black cloak was gone as well, replaced by a rough homespun jacket, complete with patches and stains, old and new.

He continued his trek around the castle, finally coming to the front gate where a few soldiers, ostensibly on guard, crouched in a circle, playing some form of dice.

One of them spared a glace over his shoulder at the old man shuffling by, but he turned right back to his game. Apparently, Asher was expected.

I waited until their attention was completely back on the game, waited until I heard the sound of rattling dice and people holding their breath, then I was past them, into the castle.

I looked around furiously for Asher. I couldn't have been more than a couple of minutes behind him, but he was nowhere to be seen.

I didn't have to be a genius to figure out what was going on. Asher had somehow incapacitated the king and stowed him away somewhere. He would now retrieve him and take him out of the castle

I had no idea how he would convince the guards that it was somehow natural for a crippled old man to be carrying a body past their dice game. I tucked myself into a corner of the castle courtyard and tried to think my way back into the chase.

From where I hid, I could see all of the main entrances to the castle. If Asher tried to take the king out of one of them, I would see him. Unfortunately, nothing in Asher's character suggested he would be taking him out one of the main entrances.

More likely, he knew some secret way out, a servant's tunnel or something that would give him a less guarded escape route.

My frustration mounted as I watched the courtyard. It was remarkably quiet for a castle courtyard. The only people I saw seemed to be in a hurry to get somewhere else.

The only person who was spending any time at all in the courtyard was a page, dressed in bright livery, who was trying in vain to keep his silks clean as he loaded a cart with what must have been leftovers from a feast.

His crude shovel was unequal to the task as he tried to scoop fruit peelings and bones into the cart. He struggled most with the carcasses of cooked animals that hadn't been eaten much.

It would have been a simple matter to grab them with his hands and throw them in the cart, but even from across the courtyard, his body language made it clear he found the thought distasteful.

Finally he managed to guide the last wobbling bit of something that looked like a turkey onto the cart and he was on his way, once again making his job much harder than it needed to be by avoiding contact with the cart as much as possible.

I watched him idly, having given up hope of finding Asher, thinking that perhaps I could slip out with the cart unnoticed. I was about to move when the page lifted his face to wipe his brow.

It was Asher.

I realized that there was more than just garbage in that cart. That cart held the king. I couldn't help but smile at Asher's ingenuity, not to mention his sense of irony, if it was intentional.

The moment was too good to interrupt, so I sat back and watched as Asher, man of violence, cringed his way through the gate, acting for all the world like he had never gotten his hands dirty. The guards never even raised their heads.

After a while I slipped back out of the castle and walked as fast as I could back to where the brothers waited for Asher. All preparations were long since finished and now they sat on a fallen tree and waited.

Even Simeon, so bold in his plan, was visibly nervous from fifty paces away. He alternated between wringing his hands and running them through his hair.

Joseph, for his part, just tapped his foot, though I don't think he was aware of it, and looked at his brother like a mother would look at a sick child. I called out to them as I got close. The last thing the two men needed right now was a surprise.

Neither offered a word of greeting, though both nodded to me. Then they went back to their hand wringing and toe tapping, looking down the road for Asher.

We didn't have to wait much longer. Asher came strolling up the road, looking for all the world like a man out enjoying the fresh air.

The burden over his shoulder, wrapped in a thick burlap sack, didn't seem to bother him in the slightest with either its weight or its import.

Simeon rose from the log and squared his shoulders. Gone was any trace of shakiness in his hands. Only his tousled hair stood testament to his earlier anxieties.

The sight of the king thrown over Asher's shoulder like a

sack of grain had solidified the reality of the situation. Like any good soldier, now that the battle was joined, he would fight on without fear or hesitation until the day was won.

Asher dumped the body without ceremony in front of the two brothers and stood calmly, as if at attention, looking from one brother to the other.

A mocking smile twitched the corner of his mouth as he saw the trepidation still in Joseph's eyes, but faded again as his eyes shifted to meet Simeon's steel gaze. Back to business.

"You've got about three hours before he starts to awaken, though he will be too groggy to remember much for another hour after that." He reported brusquely.

"Thank you, Asher." Simeon spoke in a hushed tone, giving the speech the reverence of ceremony. "You may consider any debt you owed to my family paid. You are also welcome to anything of value in our home. I left what little gold we had left under a loose floor board by the back wall. It is yours."

Simeon spoke the words like a king issuing a pardon or granting a boon. Asher responded with a snort.

"You're still young, boy, and you know nothing of the debt I owe your family. Fetching a dandy out of a stone box was closer to work for a serving boy. I still have a debt of blood that needs to be paid, and I will see it paid."

Asher leaned closer as he said the last, and the conviction of his tone sent chills down my spine. It was clear that he intended to kill for Simeon and Joseph and wouldn't be satisfied until he had.

I half expected for Simeon to argue, but he nodded.

"I don't have to explain to you what it means once he has

seen your face. Still, I won't turn down any help. Thank you.

"We are close to where we'll be staying, let's move out. I'd like to have everything in place before he wakes up."

Chapter 6

The universe holds a destiny in store for people who will not build their own, but they seldom like it.
-Musings of the Historian

Our destination was an ancient cottage tucked back in the woods. Spread around the house was a field that had once been under cultivation, but had since gone fallow.

Yellowed vines and weeds grew up the sides of the house as if nature were trying to pull the lonely little building back into the earth.

The roof had been repaired multiple times, displaying a wide range of styles. Mud, thatch, wood shingles, and even a few ceramic tiles overlapped one another in a failed attempt to keep the rain out. Even from across the field, I could see entire sections of roof missing.

Two windows, both in front, were cut out, but not covered. In spite of the rest of the house falling into ruin, the door looked to be in great shape, the hinges well-crafted and strong.

It was clear that many hands had worked on this house. Whoever had first built the house and the door had been a good craftsman, though likely poor.

Everyone who followed had patched up whatever time had taken away as best they could. For me, I couldn't help but love the house. It was the kind of place that had witnessed life and death, joy and sorrow, a hundred stories.

Simeon carried the king in and set him down on the floor. The burlap bag groaned softly at the treatment. The king was starting to find his way back from whatever Asher had done to him.

Simeon took this one opportunity to turn and face the three of us, a great sadness lurked behind the determination in his eyes.

"This is the point of no return. If the king sees any one of you, your life is forfeit, there can be no illusions or false hopes. This is absolutely your last chance."

I looked to the other two. Asher looked bored. Joseph took a dramatic step forward, squaring his shoulders as if presenting himself for sacrifice at that moment.

Simeon nodded and for a moment, the determination wavered beneath the sadness. Still, he wouldn't be turned, and the determination rose again to take its rightful place.

"Thank you." He struggled, trying to find something else to say, something to fit the moment, but there was nothing. The time for words had passed, so it turned right back to action. "Help me change his clothes."

The king grunted and mumbled as we pulled the bag off and stripped him of his fine silks. We replaced them with an over-large cotton shirt and sturdy working trousers.

If it weren't for his clean face, he could have been a young peasant sleeping off a wild night at the tavern.

It was a young face. I knew from Simeon's story that the king would be around thirty, give or take a year; but he didn't look a day past twenty. It was the pale and smooth innocence that comes of a life without care.

Tibian wasn't fat, so to speak, but he was certainly put together with rounded edges, completing the image of a man-boy who had never known hard work. The closer he drew to consciousness, the more his face scowled.

When he finally opened an eye, it was just that, one eye. It took all the energy Tibian had to drag it open. The eye flicked back and forth, taking in the room and the four somber men staring back at him.

Finally, satisfied that it could only be a bad dream, the one eye closed again and stayed closed for another five minutes. His breathing became low and steady once more. We stood silently and waited. Patience can be infinite when there is nothing else to do.

Once again, the eye opened and flicked about the room. This time, something registered and the king bolted awake, both eyes shooting open, full of panic and confusion. He shot to his feet, ready to make his escape.

Unfortunately for Tibian, he was far from ready. He took one frantic step, veering hard to his left. His next step ran right into his last one as he literally tripped over his own feet and went sprawling.

A rare smile twitched at the corner of Asher's mouth as he watched the befuddled king flounder on the floor.

"She did warn me there might be some disorientation. Might take a minute for him to figure out which way is up."

His words were prophetic as Tibian struggled to even get his hands underneath himself. He acted like a man on a heaving ship, trying hard to get his hand laid flat on the floor as if it were jumping around underneath.

Once he had his hands set, he steadied himself for a long minute, moving quickly at times to adjust for sudden movements that only he felt.

Summoning his courage, he brought up a foot and pushed himself skyward, hobbling quickly to a wall where he spun quickly to rest his back against it. With the wall at his back, he managed to stay upright.

His eyes turned to us, full of all the hatred and loathing he could muster. His jaw worked as if he wanted to spit at us, but his eyes kept shifting and I suspect we were still moving targets to his drugged mind.

"Ahlseeewalheengt!" He shrieked at us. Then realizing that his mouth hadn't quite pulled off his threat, he quickly rethought his strategy and instead shouted "Dead!" and pointed to all of us, doing his best to point at each of us in turn.

The four of us stood silently as he shouted various threats and made several attempts to leave the security of his wall.

Only Asher and I seemed to find any humor in the situation. Simeon and Joseph may as well have been carved from stone.

Finally the time came when the king stood off from his wall, his feet solid underneath him and his eyes clear and lucid. His voice dripped venom and contempt.

"You will take me back to the palace this instant or I will make sure you and everyone you have ever loved are tortured and killed for this treason!"

This was what Simeon had been waiting for. He sprang forward to slam Tibian against the wall, putting his own face mere inches from the young king's.

"Look at my face!" Simeon shouted, though he could have been heard with the softest whisper. The king, to his credit, did not shrink from the verbal assault.

"Take a good look, memorize its features and know my name. I am Simeon, son of Ander. Behind me are my brother and my friends. We were all dead men the moment you saw our faces. Indeed, the only way we could ever hope to see old age is... to... kill... you!"

Simeon punctuated each of his last words by slamming the king against the wall, bouncing his head off the rough boards and pressing the air from his lungs.

The king's knees went wobbly and Simeon let him slump back down to the ground. He crouched down and spoke softly.

"Perhaps his majesty would take that into consideration when making threats, attempting escape, or disobeying when he is given orders."

Tibian snapped his head up, ready to argue, and met Simeon's eyes. The anger froze on his face and melted away as the reality of what had been said sunk in. Flickers of fear began to chase across his face as Simeon held his gaze like a hawk staring down a mouse.

"You... you wouldn't..." It was almost a whimper, a voiced hope more than an argument. Simeon smiled wickedly and patted the soft cheek as if he were comforting a sick child.

"Oh no, my dear king, I certainly wouldn't. I don't seem to have it in me." The king sniffled and cocked his head suspiciously. Simeon's tone was far from kindly.

"But you see, I wouldn't be the one doing it. Do you

recognize anyone else behind me, your majesty? Look closely."

The king finally broke eye contact with Simeon to look behind him. First he looked at me, but moved quickly to Joseph, his eyes flicking for a blink back to Simeon, as if confirming the family link.

When his eyes flicked back, they landed on Asher and held. He kept looking at Asher, dark suspicions lining his face as he shook his head.

"No? Nobody you could put a name to?" Simeon prodded. The king shook his head again, but continued to look at Asher. "I suppose not, but he doesn't really need a name, does he? You certainly seem to have gotten the idea.

"Most people say they can see it in the eyes, the deadness, the savagery. For me, I see it in the hands. Something about those bones and sinews speaks to me of blood and torn flesh. What do you think, your majesty?"

The king looked back to Simeon, horror written plainly on his face, but he did not speak.

"Oh well, I guess it doesn't matter. The point is you see it, and if you have even half a wit you can see your own death in those eyes, by those hands.

"Should you ever have a fleeting moment where you forget what you are feeling right now, then remember his name. You are looking at Asher."

The king recognized the name and went even paler around the edges. Still Simeon pressed on, pretending he hadn't seen the recognition.

"No? Nothing? Strange, most people have heard his name around. He was kind of a big deal during the war. I guess you weren't around for that part."

Simeon turned his head slightly in Asher's direction while still maintaining eye contact with the king. "Hey Asher, maybe his majesty would recognize another name. What was it the Marauders called you?"

"Gholost." Asher responded simply.

"Strange name, Asher. Any idea what it means?"

"It means Hunger."

"My, my, aren't you full of surprises." Simeon said in a tone that made it clear he was anything but surprised. Through it all, he held the king's eyes with his own. "Why would a people name you Hunger?"

"Hunger consumes and destroys men, it can never be completely satisfied, and it cannot be escaped from." Asher spoke the words with a dark pride that left no doubt that he had earned the title time and time again.

Any bravado had long since drained from the king and he unconsciously drew his knees closer to his chest, pulling himself into a fetal position as if expecting a blow at any moment. At that moment, he looked for all the world like a child who had seen his first monster.

I guess in many ways that's exactly what had happened.

Simeon stood back up, looking down at the broken king. Now that the king's eyes weren't on him, he looked sad, but when he spoke, his voice was as hard as ever.

"For the next couple days, you will get to know hunger. As you work, you will be guided. As you resist, you will starve. As you flee, you will bleed."

Simeon turned on his heel and walked out of the house,

the rest of us following quickly behind him. I closed the door behind me with one last glance at the king sitting in the dirt, his head in his hands.

Chapter 7

While we build our lives with thousands of repetitions and mundane habits, in the end, our lives are defined by only a few shining moments.

-Musings of the Historian

The first day was a hard one for the young king. The night before he had feasted with his close friends and had fallen asleep in a drunken stupor. I suspect his breakfast back at the castle was sumptuous and extravagant.

Undoubtedly he ate in bed every morning. I closed my eyes and pictured the scene as servants rushed the delicious meal into his bedroom to find him gone.

Confusion would feed whispers and hurried searches through the castle. Finally, the confusion would fall to panic. The whispers and quiet searches would give way to shouts and orders. The searches would become thorough and widespread.

Once the panic had burned itself out, fiery coals of fear would settle into people's hearts as new questions of "what if...?" were explored within unsteady hearts.

This is when things would get dangerous inside the castle, for few things are more unpredictable than a mass of scared people.

With any luck, there would be a strong hand within the castle who would hold things together and decide that it was best if the country thought the king were merely away for a time while they sorted things out.

On the other hand, if they weren't that lucky, factions would quickly form in the castle as people vied to secure their own positions.

The worst case scenario would have these splinters spreading through the whole nation, with civil war breaking out before the king had a chance to get good and hungry.

But all of these dark predictions seemed quite out of place in the quiet woods where we sat quietly and watched the cottage and its miserable occupant.

The king would poke his head up at one of the two windows and then dart back down as if he expected an arrow.

We all sat together, though no one spoke. The hours passed that way in silence. The sun rose higher and higher in the sky, chasing the last of the chill from the morning air.

Three of us spent the entire morning motionless. Simeon was lost in thought, contemplating the risks he had exposed his country to. Asher was a statue, a gargoyle posted to guard a king. He scarcely blinked.

As for me, I scarcely notice the passage of time like most people do. Every moment is an eternity and years pass in the blink of an eye. The hazards of immortality, I'm afraid, include a kind of madness when it comes to the passage of time.

That left only poor Joseph to feel the slow crawl of the morning. Every ten minutes or so he would fidget and glance toward the sun, or tilt his head at some new angle toward the house, as if by doing so he could see what the king was up to.

He opened his mouth several times to ask some question,

or try and start up a conversation. Each time his mouth popped back closed again. I knew the feeling. What does one talk about at such a time?

He looked to Simeon often enough, but obviously couldn't bring himself to break his brother's reverie.

He looked to me and the helplessness only grew. He didn't know me or trust me well enough for a deep conversation; and the scene simply did not lend itself to idle getting-to-know-you banter.

That left Asher. And though the young man would never admit it, he was still too intimidated by the dark figure to question him. Even though a wolf may fight on your side, that does not make him a dog.

So the poor boy was left to fidget and peer at the sun as it began its descent through the sky.

I imagine the only person in the area who was more uncomfortable was the king. I would bet anything that the spoiled man-boy had never missed a single meal his entire life.

For such a person, missing a meal was immediately uncomfortable. Missing two would be dizzying. By three missed meals, the king would likely be entertaining melodramatic thoughts of death by hunger and the wasting away of his limbs.

As the sun started to nestle down on the mountains, the king found his courage again and shouted out the window.

"Food! I need food, you animals! I'm no good to you dead!"

I smiled. It appeared my prediction of melodrama was spot on. Joseph looked anxiously to his brother. I doubt he had any concerns about the king's well-being, but was getting desperate to have something happen. Anything would do. His fidgeting had taken on a manic feel in the last couple hours.

Still, there was no relief for Joseph, or for the king. Both were ignored, though the king shouted several more demands over the next couple hours before giving up.

When darkness fell, Joseph finally broke and stood up, hurrying around to set up a camp. His bottled energy from the day made for quick work and soon Simeon turned his back to the cottage to stretch his hands towards the small fire Joseph had whipped up.

Asher repositioned himself to a spot by the fire where he could feel its warmth, but still maintain a clear field of vision to his target across the field.

Fire has a wondrous effect on people. Watching it flickering fills the eyes with light and the mind with thoughts and emotions. For Joseph, it appeared that the fire gave him courage, because he finally broke his day-long silence and spoke to Asher, of all people.

"So what is the debt you owe my father? What does a man like yourself value so highly that you would put your life on the line for us?"

Asher was quiet for a long time, and Joseph gave up and let the matter drop, poking a stick absentmindedly into the fire. He was standing up to move somewhere else when Asher spoke.

"It was during the Marauder war. We had organized, they had organized. For the first time, war became about large battles where hundreds of men died, rather than small skirmishes where one force chased the other off.

"I was part of the regular army then, a captain of a squadron of handpicked men. We were the first into every battle and our reputation was formidable. I had chosen men who were like me and trained them to kill as I did.

"I gloried in it. I let the bloodlust of battle and the respect of men wash over me like a tide. Men everywhere knew my name, I lived large off gifts and tribute from all around me. The army camp was my home and my life.

"Even my beloved, Eliana, traveled with me as a camp follower. She was wiser than I and chose to ignore the fame that comes with blood. She worked with the other women, cooking and nursing. She found her glory in life, not death.

"It was a trivial battle that changed my life. The numbers involved were not impressive and the ground we fought for was not critical. Still, any battle for me was more than worth the effort.

"True to form, I brought all my men together and plunged into the heart of the battle. Until the battle's end, I had no idea what had gone on behind me.

"As the rest of the army formed up and charged to the flank, a small band of Marauders, just five men, ran into the camp. The general ordered the men to ignore the smaller party and push on to the real battle.

"Strategically, it was the right decision. No general worth his salt would split his force over such a trivial matter when the men would simply dart off and then attack somewhere else, drawing the men on into ambush.

"For your father, however, it wasn't so simple, he saw the innocent lives who had been left undefended there at the camp when the army marched. He disobeyed the order and abandoned the army to run back to camp.

"As my wife told the story, she had already been knocked

to the ground and a Marauder stood above her when your father barreled into the man, knocking him to the ground and dispatching him with a quick thrust of his dagger.

"The kill was not clean, however, and the man let out a scream before he succumbed. The other four Marauders closed in quickly. Had it been me, I would have killed all four and none would have even counted it as an act of bravery, least of all me.

"As it was, your father was just a soldier; skilled but inexperienced. He was wounded by each in their turn. Each time their blades got to him, he returned cut for cut. In the end, his heart was simply greater.

"They fell to their wounds or ran off. When the army returned, we found the women treating your father in a puddle of his own blood, they being unable to drag him from the mud.

"I rode into camp next to the general, having been the hero of the battle once again. When the general saw that Ander had disobeyed orders, he lifted his arm and ordered his men to take your father into custody for court martial.

"Without another thought, I took the general's arm; cut it off at the elbow. The camp erupted. The men most loyal to the general sprang to help him and to take me down.

"The first two to try were cut down for their trouble. Then I was off the horse and my men were around me. If the whole army had rushed us, they might have eventually succeeded against us, though there is some doubt, as my men's loyalty was absolute.

"As it was, most of the army had no idea what to do, most were raw recruits and took orders from me as often as the general.

58

"In no time at all, my men and I had formed a circle around your father and the general himself had called his men to stop attacking us. He made his decisions like a true military man.

"The decision to leave the camp and the decision to arrest your father were based in logic. He now made another decision based on what he saw before him.

"If he pressed the attack, his men would die. They were no match for the death squad I had built around myself. My men were every bit as lethal as I was. Beyond that, there wasn't a single one of them who wasn't willing to die for me.

"Trying to bring the army in for an attack would force a choice in loyalty that he might not win. In the end, even the general was a greater man than I.

"He apologized. He spoke through clenched teeth, but he forgave your father his insubordination and praised his valor. He then ordered me from the army, stripped of all rank and entitlements.

"My men were offered places as common soldiers if they would lay down their arms. I ordered them to take the offer. They did not dare disobey me in my wrath.

"I left the regular army that day. I moved my wife to a cottage in the woods, where she would be safe. I made sure she had everything she could possibly need. Once that was done, I took off on my own to fight the Marauders."

Here Asher's eyes took on something close to emotion as he spoke of his wife.

"Looking back on it now, I should have stayed with her. It is my only regret that I didn't take the time I was given and gather more warm memories."

Asher fell silent and stared into the fire. Joseph had enough sense not to prod any further.

So the four of us stared into one fire.

I saw magic.

Joseph saw courage.

Simeon saw peace.

Asher saw demons.

Chapter 8

Animal rage is scary, but not as scary as control.

–Musings of the Historian

The night passed simply enough. It was cold and damp. We took turns keeping watch over the small house. When it was my turn, I crept in close enough to listen to the king's teeth chattering within. I didn't chance a look, but I am certain he didn't sleep a wink that night. Too cold, too hungry, too afraid.

The morning was brisk and clear, and I couldn't help but feel some anticipation. I think Joseph's attitude was beginning to rub off on me.

As soon as the sun was clear of the mountains, the king stepped out of his ragged prison. He took a moment at the door, blinking at the sun and brushing off his clothes as best he could.

When he was satisfied, he drew himself up as tall as he could and stepped regally into the field. He stopped after a few steps and announced.

"I would like to speak to the man who has kidnapped me! What would you have me do?"

From his bearing, it was plain that he wanted to come across as proud and royal. Unfortunately, his voice was hoarse from the long night and broke twice during his short speech.

There were muddy tracks on his face where dirt had clung to tears in the night. Still, he stood bravely, searching the tree line through bloodshot eyes.

I half expected Simeon to ignore him again, as he had the previous day. Instead, he hurried to his feet and nodded for us to follow as he walked out to meet the king.

To my astonishment, when he got to within three paces of the king, he dropped to one knee and bowed his head. Joseph and I fumbled through bows of our own. Asher stood silent.

Simeon rose and spoke simply.

"A man should be able to feed himself."

Then he walked over to the old well that stood by the house and drew up the bucket. This had been one of the preparations made beforehand. The thick rope and heavy wooden bucket were both new.

The water was clear and cold and Simeon poured water from the large bucket into a pottery cup that had been placed there earlier. He then pushed the big bucket back over the edge and let it fall back into the well with a distant splash.

He returned to the king with the cup brimming over and proceeded to drink it dry right in front of him. Tibian's lips worked instinctively as he gazed longingly at the water.

When the last of the water was gone, Simeon gave an exaggerated sigh of pleasure and wiped his forearm over the drips hanging from his chin.

He then handed the empty cup to the king and gestured to the well.

"All the water you can drink, brought to you by the strength of your own arm."

The king glared daggers at Simeon, gripping the handle of the cup as if he were about to throw it at his captor. In the end, however, thirst won out over pride and he walked over to the well.

Where Simeon had easily raised the heavy bucket of water, Tibian struggled at the rope, especially when he had to change hands.

When he got the bucket to the top and had to hold it with one hand while he shifted the bucket to the edge of the well, the result was comical.

He already had one foot up against the well wall to help pull on the heavy rope. Even when he managed to get the rope anchored to his side with one hand, every time he tried to lean forward to grab the handle, the bucket would lower just out of his reach.

His face grew red with shame as he went through several rounds of this like a dog trying to catch his own tail. Mercifully, he finally latched his fingers on the handle and let go of the rope to grab at it with both hands.

The quick motion almost had the king diving head first into the well. He managed to set his feet against the side of the well and haul the bucket up onto the ledge, sloshing water down the front of himself.

He wisely decided against trying to pour water from the bucket, as Simeon had done. He instead opted to dip the cup into the cold water.

He sipped slowly at first, his throat sore. Then he was pulling frantically at the cup, drinking as much as he could hold.

Water sloshed out from around his mouth and down his chest, though it couldn't make him any wetter than he already was. He stumbled back to Simeon, all pretenses of dignity washed away with the well water.

Simeon was ready for him and presented him with a withered leaf. Had it been fresh, it would have been a dark green and shaped broader at the base, moving closer together until it came to a point, with serrated edges.

As it was, only someone experienced could have connected the limp piece of yellow matter to a potato plant. Simeon announced as much.

"This is the leaf of a potato plant. Even though this farm hasn't been worked in years, the plants have kept growing on their own. If you find plants that look like this, there are potatoes underneath.

"You might have to dig deep to find any that weren't destroyed by mold or frost, but I'm confident that you'll figure it out, now that you're properly motivated."

Having finished his speech, Simeon handed over the leaf with all the ceremony of a dignitary presenting a jeweled crown. The king looked positively sick.

I imagine it was a mix between having drank too much water and the dawning realization that he would have to root around in the dirt like a pig if he wanted to eat.

Simeon turned and left again, the rest of us following. The king numbly began to follow us, but Asher turned swiftly and gave him a hard shove in the chest.

The king staggered backward a couple of steps before losing his feet and crashing down hard on his back. He was still lying there when we reached the tree line.

When he finally rose, he paced and shouted hoarse threats at the woods until his voice gave out and his knees shook from hunger.

I imagine that for him, going on two full days without anything to eat was quite an ordeal, though I'm sure many of his subjects had gone much longer without anything to eat so their children wouldn't go to bed hungry.

Giving one last roar of frustration at the woods, he finally poked around at the ground until he found an old potato plant and started scraping away at the ground with his fingers. He paused occasionally to inspect lumps and throw them away.

Finally he found one that didn't get thrown away, though he stared at it for a long time before closing his eyes and biting into the old potato.

He chewed only a couple of times before spitting it out, retching in disgust and rubbing his mouth on his sleeve.

He sunk back on his haunches, and then plopped down to a sitting position. He drew his knees to his chest and planted his face on them. His shoulders shook occasionally and I suspect, had I been a touch closer, I would have heard him sobbing.

He stayed that way for an hour or two as the sun beat down on his shoulders. Time had crept away from me again and I noticed that it was already afternoon.

His head popped up with a jerk, and I realized that he had drifted off to sleep and had just popped back into his harsh new reality. His scowl was evident, even from the tree line.

He reached over and picked up the potato he had discarded. He rubbed it on the sleeve of his shirt like he was polishing an apple.

He kept at it, hoping it would improve the appearance if it were cleaner. It was a lost cause. In the end, there was nothing left to do but bite, so he bit.

He took a smaller chunk this time, and only chewed it three or four times before swallowing it. He took a moment to flash what could only have been an obscene gesture at the woods before taking another small bite.

In no time at all, his potato was gone and he was crawling back to his dig site, scratching deeper in the soil for another potato. There were none left at that plant that were edible, so he moved on to the next.

As luck would have it, while digging around that plant, he chanced upon a thin, sharp rock. Now that the king had himself a shovel, he was tearing at the ground like he was hunting for treasure.

He found another potato and ate it, pausing only once to gag at the strong earthy flavor. The next potato he found was set to the side. It was soon joined by more potatoes as the king committed to his new position as a gatherer of tubers.

In no time at all, a significant pile had formed and the king crouched over them as if someone would come and take them from him.

He ate three more potatoes before scooping the rest of them into his shirt and carrying them into the house. He emerged looking taller and went again to the well where the bucket still sat on the edge. He dipped his cup again and took a good long drink.

When the cup was empty, he raised it in a defiant salute towards the woods. With his other hand, he repeated the rude gesture from before. Then he stomped back into the house and we didn't see him again until that night.

Deep in the dark hours, the good king Tibian tried to

escape. Some combination of old potatoes and clear water had given him his attitude back and he made his break under the cover of darkness.

It was during Simeon's watch and he leaned over to touch Asher's shoulder. Asher asked no questions, but rose from the ground and disappeared into the woods like a ghost.

In no time at all, the king's screams and protests were heard coming from the dark wood, drawing ever closer.

Joseph had finally woken up and Simeon nodded to the two of us to follow as he took a few steps into the clearing.

We were there less than a minute when the king burst through the tree line, barely keeping his feet under him as he was shoved from behind by Asher.

He managed to keep his balance until he was almost in front of us. Then Asher caught up to him and shoved him hard to the ground face first, placing his knee between the king's shoulder blades and pressing until the king whimpered softly. He looked up pleadingly at Simeon.

"A man should be able to bear pain with dignity."

The king's expression went quickly through confusion, fear, and then outright horror as Asher slowly pulled a knife from his boot. The scene looked like it was all happening in slow motion, but it wasn't a trick of suspense. The truth was that Asher was moving incredibly slowly, like a glacier.

The king's eyes were as round as saucers as he stared at the knife glinting in the moonlight. He shuddered and thrashed wildly, but all his efforts did nothing to faze Asher as his knife crept towards Tibian's right shoulder.

The struggle had pulled his shirt off his shoulder and his

bare flesh looked ethereal in the pale night lighting.

Tibian gasped as the cold tip of the blade touched the top of his shoulder, almost by his neck. The gasp turned scream as the tip kept pressing down until a black drop of blood started to pool around the tip. Tibian gave one more wild thrash as he screamed, but there was nothing for it.

With the same agonizing slowness, Asher began to pull the blade to the side, progressing along the shoulder, heading towards the arm.

The dark dribble of blood followed the tip as it crept across his flesh. Tibian gave up thrashing for fear of making it worse. He pressed his shoulder hard towards the ground as if trying to get it further away from Asher.

Still the blade continued its slow plod. The cut wasn't deep by any standard, little more than a scratch, but I could feel only horror as I watched the king plant his face in the ground and scream at his helplessness.

He raised his head. His tears and saliva had turned to mud from the dirt. In the eerie lighting, it looked as if he were bleeding out of his mouth and eyes.

Still, the moon was at our backs, it would have been impossible for him to see our faces at all. In any event, no one made a sound or a move to help him, and he turned his face back to the ground, breathing heavily.

When it finally ended, the king sported a cut on his shoulder that oozed blood slowly down to his shirt. The cut was only about as long as the distance from wrist to fingertip, but the process had taken at least three full minutes. Asher's control was inhuman.

As soon as he finished, he pushed himself off of Tibian and stood back up. The king, for his part, did not show any particular desire to rise.

He stayed where he was, keeping his face pressed tightly against the cold ground. I took a moment to steal a look at the others.

Joseph looked positively sick, and was doing a thorough job of avoiding eye contact with anyone. Simeon looked as determined as ever, but I could swear I saw a hint of a tear shining at the corner of his eye as he looked down on his king.

Asher looked bored.

I think Simeon wanted to say something, but didn't trust himself to maintain a steady voice. The silence began to grow a little awkward. I decided I might as well do the job myself.

I do my best to never interfere with the decisions that move a story forward, but nothing says I can't move the plot along a bit when it starts to drag.

"Would you like some help back to your house, your majesty?

The other three looked at me curiously, but no one objected. Tibian snorted from the ground and I took it as a yes. I took him under the arm, being careful not to have anything rub up against his cut.

Joseph moved to the other side and together we helped King Tibian to his feet. As soon as his feet were under him, he shook us off. He turned to face Simeon, even though he probably couldn't see much of his face in the dark.

"If you think you can break me, you're a fool!" The young king spat the words at Simeon. "You talk of manhood like you're trying to teach me something; but you stand by and have your dirty work done for you by your mad dog.

"I will play your twisted game and I will win. I will live to see the day when I stand above you with my boot on your throat. But if the time comes that you decide to kill me, I hope you have the courage to do it yourself."

The king finished his speech and stomped back toward his hovel, muttering to himself in the darkness. Simeon turned to watch him go and for the first time, I got a full look at his face in the moonlight. A broad grin stretched across his face.

Simeon was happy.

Chapter 9

If you would see a man's heart, knock him down. Then observe how he rises. If you would see his soul, do it a thousand times more.

-Musings of the Historian

When we got back to our own camp, Joseph rounded on his older brother.

"What was that?! I understand we need him to learn some things, but what could he possibly learn from torture? How could you justify this? Is this the sort of people we are?"

Simeon was a little taken aback by the verbal onslaught, but was still feeling too pleased with how the evening had gone to let his brother's tirade throw him off.

"Did you see him?" Simeon didn't look directly at his brother, but aimed the question at the group. Joseph looked confused and angry at being ignored.

"I saw him fine, Simeon. I saw a man get held down and cut while we watched. You even commanded it! Did you know this was going to happen?"

Simeon nodded.

"Did you plan this?"

Another nod.

"I have followed you this far because I trust you. I know that you are a good man, but I can't believe that a good man would allow what I saw tonight.

"I think I deserve an answer or two. Or perhaps you would at least like to explain yourself to our new friend. After all, you brought him along to judge us. I can only imagine what kind of judgment he would pass right now."

Simeon thought for a few seconds before speaking, gathering his words.

"Yes, Joseph. You saw him tonight, just as I did. You saw a man held down and cut. You saw him scream and writhe from the pain.

"And then… then you saw him rise, filthy and bloody, and throw it all back in my face. He spoke his heart even though it might mean more torture or his death. He was noble.

"I planned this tonight and I have planned more. All of my planning revolves around building a strong king, one who could stand and protect our people.

"You already know this, but one thing you may not have realized is that men only grow under pressure. You can't build muscle lying in bed. You need resistance. You need pain and struggle.

"For any of this to mean anything, the king must understand good and evil. He must feel the darkness that exists in a man's heart that he may learn to defend against it.

"I have tried to be a good man all my life. But tonight, our king did not need a good man. He needed a cruel man. He needed to feel coldness and pain press on him and try to crush his soul so he could push back.

"Tonight I saw my king and I promise you he is worth it. He can be who we need him to be. Right now, my king needs me to be a villain. So a villain I shall be."

I had my eyes on Joseph. His hands ran through his hair as he struggled to reconcile the deeper meaning of what his brother said with what he still felt in his heart.

It was the expected reaction. Seeing what I expected to see from Joseph made me that much more unprepared for what I thought I would never see.

Asher was crying.

It wasn't crying like you'd expect from most people. If anything, his face only grew more impassive, as if it were carved from stone, but there were tears on his face. He stared at Simeon with ice cold eyes.

"I hope you know what you're doing, boy." Asher's voice betrayed none of the emotion he was feeling. "I know better than any man the line you're trying to walk. I can tell you now that good intentions don't mean a good night's sleep."

Nothing more was said that night.

In the morning, the king once again stood out where he had the previous morning, gnawing on an old potato. He was waiting for us.

Simeon led us out. Joseph walked to his right hand, Asher to his left. For my part, I always managed to look like someone who happened to be walking in the same direction by chance.

"These things taste like moldy dirt." The king started without preamble or pleasantries. "How do I get better food?"

"I'll make you a deal, your majesty. I will provide you with seeds. If you can get a row of any kind of plant to sprout, I will give you the end product, an advance on future effort.

"In the meantime, perhaps you should try cooking your

potatoes, I know I prefer them that way."

"Ah, but of course!" The king exclaimed bitterly. "Why didn't I think of that? As far as that goes, why didn't I think to build a fire last night when I was freezing to death? I don't know how!"

The confession was a hard one for him to make. Anyone could tell he didn't want to give Simeon the satisfaction of seeing him struggle.

His pride was strong. Even as he admitted his weakness, he threw back his shoulders and said it as if it were a challenge.

"A man should know how to make a fire." Simeon shrugged.

If the king had had a knife at that moment, I'm sure he would have gladly cut Simeon's heart from his chest. The hatred burned in his eyes like hot coals, but he managed to maintain control.

"Well I don't. Somehow I never found the time amid ruling my kingdom."

"Perhaps you should try it." Simeon suggested. "I mean starting a fire, of course, though heaven knows you haven't tried ruling your kingdom either."

The king bristled at the insult, turned, and walked back to the house. We went back to camp.

Later that day, Simeon smiled from the tree line as he listened to the sounds of rock on rock, barely noticeable above a steady stream of cursing that flowed from the hut.

"Joseph, go teach him how to start a fire. I think he's about ready for some guidance."

Joseph nodded and jumped to his feet, eager for

something to do. He had been bored out of his mind for almost the entire process.

No doubt he had expected the process of kidnapping and training up a king to be dangerous and exciting. No one ever realizes that even the greatest works are primarily acts of , patience.

Without being asked, I fell in behind him. No one questioned me. My place in the group was a strange one. I was expected to be a part of everything, but not really to participate.

The most I had done so far was to take my turn at watch. Even then, it was only with orders to wake Simeon or Asher if I saw anything.

Joseph set to the task enthusiastically, moving briskly to get the blood flowing back through his legs. He may have been a bit overeager, however, and didn't quite consider the consequences of poking one's head into a house where someone has been failing to start a fire for over an hour.

Joseph stepped in and immediately had a rock thrown at his head. An instinctive flinch got him out of the rock's path, but only barely. The rock bounced harmlessly off the door frame, only to be followed moments later by another rock.

This time, Joseph wasn't quick enough as his eyes adjusted to the dim lighting in the small house. The rock hit him on his arm and he yelped and rubbed at his arm.

"Hey! Enough of that! I came to help." Joseph's tone was angry enough that the king stopped looking around for another rock to peer at his new arrival.

"Will you help me escape?"

"Uh, no. I meant I came to help you make a fire. As you

work, you will be guided." Joseph mimicked the same line his older brother had used on the first day of the king's captivity.

The king's shoulders sank. He gestured lamely toward his makings. He had gathered dried grass from outside and had been smacking two rocks together to make sparks.

"I suppose I should take whatever help I can get. This is ridiculous. I got the driest grass I could find, but even when I get sparks to land on them, nothing happens. What am I doing wrong?"

The usual pride and anger that laced the king's voice when talking to Simeon was absent when talking to his brother. Around Joseph, he was just a man having a hard time lighting a fire. Joseph, for his part, was more than happy to instruct.

"We'll get to that in a moment. First of all, what would you have done if your plan had worked?"

"I would have a fire, I don't see what you're getting at." The king shook his head in puzzlement at Joseph's strange question.

"Do this for me, I want you to picture in your mind the spark catching in the grass and springing to flame. Now just keep imagining. Let the scene play out. My brother says a good imagination is the best preparation a man can have."

The king's anger flared for a moment at the mention of Simeon, but he looked to his pile of grass and focused on it, playing the scene through in his mind, as Joseph had instructed. His eyes lifted and ran over the room frantically. He understood what his new teacher had been driving at.

"I don't have any wood in here." He stated simply, having realized that his pile of grass would burn itself out in moments, long before he could bring back any more fuel. Joseph nodded, proud of his new pupil.

"A fire is like a growing creature. When it is young, it has to be fed soft things, like a baby. As it grows stronger, it can handle more and more, but you must never give it more, or less, than it is ready for. Let's go get bigger logs first, and then we'll go smaller, ok?"

The king nodded and rose to his feet. He was already responding well to Joseph. It was becoming clear that Simeon had planned this as well.

It was true that the king needed an enemy to make him strong. But it was just as true that the king would need a friend as well, or he would become hard. A hard king could easily be worse than a weak king.

Days of abuse and neglect had prepared the king for the introduction of someone like Joseph. Someone who would be kind to the king, but who wouldn't deviate from the plan out of loyalty to his brother. My respect for Simeon as a strategist was growing.

We all headed outside and the king started off enthusiastically toward a nearby tree, pulling at one of the lower branches, trying to break it off. Joseph stopped him.

"Living trees have water running through them, sire. Even if you have a fire strong enough to burn green wood, it will make too much smoke for it to be worth it. You would smoke yourself clear out of the house if you tried to burn that.

"Let's head over to the tree line and find a fallen tree. Those are usually well dried. Also, on certain kinds of trees, branches near the bottom die off and dry out still on the tree. A good rule of thumb is that if it breaks with a snap, it will make good firewood. If it bends, it's still too green."

The king nodded, absorbing the new information. It didn't take us long to find a dead tree. Bugs and other small creatures had made their homes under the sheltering trunk. The old branches stuck up in the air like the bones of a skeleton. When the king reached out and pulled on one, it snapped off with a satisfying crack.

Joseph and I jumped in to help and soon we each had a large armful of wooden branches ranging from twigs to logs as thick as a man's forearm. As we lacked an axe, that was as big as we could gather.

We dropped off our branches at the house. The king went to take them inside, but Joseph stopped him. He informed the king that bringing a host of insects inside a house would always be a bad idea. Instead, he put him to work outside, breaking up the branches and twigs and sorting them into three piles.

The first was the heaviest logs, piled up on top of one another so the bottom ones would stay somewhat dry should it rain. The next was smaller branches, about as thick around as a thumb. The last pile was the tiny twigs, most of them barely bigger than toothpicks.

"Logs, kindling, twigs." Joseph pointed to each pile and named it in turn. Tibian nodded along, a willing student. "Now for the tinder."

"And what is tinder?" Working with us had made the king comfortable with asking questions.

"Tinder is what catches the spark. A spark is the seed of a fire. It is far too small and weak to do anything without help, so we must provide it a home to protect it. We must give it a soft nest, the softer the better."

The king looked around, puzzling it out. Finally an idea occurred to him and he started picking at the frayed edge of his cotton shirt.

Once he had managed to pull out a few threads, he untwisted them until they were fibers, then he rolled the whole mess between his hands until it was a white ball of fluff.

He handed it out to Joseph for approval. Joseph nodded, a smile on his face.

"That will work nicely. Though you should learn where to get it from nature. That way you won't have to destroy your only clothes getting fires started. Several trees have soft bark underneath their outer bark that does great for tinder once its dried.

"Also, if you are by water, cattails have soft fluff at the end of them that catches a spark wonderfully. Let's go inside and I'll show you how this will be done. Bring some twigs and kindling."

The king moved willingly and quickly. He had become completely caught up in his quest to attain fire for himself. No doubt his futile efforts from before had served to add value to the knowledge being shared.

Joseph moved quickly, but explained himself as he went, taking materials from the king as he spoke.

"The spark will catch on the cotton and embers will start to spread. When a flame finally starts, we'll want it to catch in the grass, so we form a nest of grass around our cotton, like so, so we'll be ready.

"Next is our twigs and kindling. We need to create a pyramid of twigs with a space beneath it to place our burning grass once it has caught.

"Then make a larger pyramid of kindling over the top of your twig pyramid. The tinder lights the grass, the grass lights the twigs, and the twigs light the kindling, see?"

Once the basic preparations had been made, Joseph stood back to let the king take control of the final process. Tibian retrieved the rocks he had thrown at Joseph earlier and crouched over the nest of cotton and grass.

His hour of effort had at least taught him how to produce a good shower of sparks, though it still took several attempts before one finally caught in the cotton and started to slowly spread.

"Pick up the nest and breathe on it softly." Joseph's instructions were a mere whisper at the king's ear. "Blow too hard and it will go out, just breathe. And make sure there is always fuel right above the ember, fire always travels up."

The king followed the instructions precisely, breathing on the tiny ember as if whispering a secret.

Wisps of smoke began to creep through the grass as the ember grew brighter, eating up more cotton and beginning to singe nearby strands of grass.

When the flame finally burst into life, it was so sudden that the king almost dropped the nest. It went directly from being a ball of grass and smoke to being a ball of flame, as if every dry bit of grass had ignited at once.

The king thrust the flaming nest under the pyramid of twigs.

"Blow a bit harder now. More air will make more heat, and the twigs need to catch before the grass burns out." Joseph spoke quickly and the king laid belly down on the dirt floor to blow long steady breaths at the small pocket of fire.

It flared to life under his care and in no time at all, the kindling was burning brightly, small crackling sounds popping whenever the fire found pockets of sap in the wood.

The king pushed himself up on his knees and stared at the fire he had created. From the look on his face, he may as well have been looking at his first born child.

"Go get more kindling and three logs." Joseph prompted and the king scampered out of the hovel to obey. He returned with the wood and a triumphant smile.

Following Joseph's instructions, he piled more kindling on the fire, building it up stronger and starting a base of hot coals. The logs were placed carefully, so as not to crush the young fire.

When the logs had caught fire, we all sat back on the ground and watched the flames. He had built it away from the fireplace, but there were so many holes in the roof, the lack of a chimney wasn't much of a problem.

We left him there in front of his fire. Later in the day he would try to cook his potatoes and fail miserably, but for now, he was fully caught up in the trance of the fire and the satisfaction of doing something for himself.

Chapter 10

Creation is an act of emotion.

-Musings of the Historian

The next morning, the king planted himself in the same spot, awaiting what had become his traditional standoff with Simeon. When we marched out to meet him, Simeon hid his hands behind his back, walking like a general inspecting the troops.

"You promised me seeds." The king started out. Simeon rifled through his pockets and threw several packets out onto the ground, keeping his left hand behind him the whole time.

"There's carrots, corn, and broccoli there. Should be enough to get you started, if you can get even one to sprout."

Tibian ignored the taunt and moved on to his next demand.

"I want some salt for the potatoes, and I need digging tools if I am to plant these."

This seemed to be what Simeon was waiting for. Reaching behind his belt with his right hand, he drew out a short, single-edged knife.

With a flick of his wrist, he threw it into the ground at the king's feet by the seed packets. The king still hadn't moved to pick anything up.

It seemed that having his first decent night's sleep,

warmed by the fire, had reminded him that a king doesn't stoop or bow in front of his captors.

Then Simeon drew out his left hand, where he held one of the blocks of wood he had picked out so carefully and threw it on the ground with the rest of the supplies.

"A man should be able to make something beautiful." he pronounced solemnly. "Carve me something and I will trade you salt and digging tools for it."

The king's reaction surprised me. He recoiled as if he had been slapped. His self-control wavered and once again he glared at Simeon with unbridled hatred.

Though it may have been a trick of the morning light, I would tell you that his eyes seemed to tear up at the sight of the block of wood.

"Get out of here!" He hissed the words like someone would pronounce a curse. Simeon nodded and we all left, leaving the king standing among his new treasures and promises.

"What was that about?" Joseph asked as soon as we were out of earshot. "The thing with the wood block, I mean."

"We can't very well teach him a full craft, but we can't be giving him everything, either. So I gave him a path to work for what he can't make or gather himself."

"No, I get all that." Joseph pressed. "I mean why did he get all emotional like that? Did I miss something? You knew something when you got those wooden blocks."

Simeon considered this for a moment.

"I didn't exactly know, but I guessed wood carving would hit closer to home for him than anything else I could offer.

"You see, father told us a story of the king visiting a war

camp he was a part of once.

"For some reason, it stuck in my mind that he mentioned that Stephan gave small carved animals to a couple children who traveled with the camp.

"A man who would carve things for strangers would certainly carve them for his own children. I'd gamble that our young king played with toys carved by his father when he was a small child.

"I didn't know it would strike such a strong reaction in him, though. It's encouraging to see that he holds the memory of his father so close."

The next morning, the king did not stand outside to meet Simeon, though we watched from a distance as he drew water, gathered wood, and dug for potatoes. For long stretches of time, he would stay inside.

The next several days were the same. Though no attempts were made at escape, Simeon was beginning to look worried.

"He'd better not get used to this." He grumbled one day. "I wanted him to know the life of his lowliest peasant; but if he comes to accept it, we're doomed."

His fears proved unfounded as the king once again stood outside waiting for us, four days since we had last spoken. Rather than speak first, as he had done the other times, he threw a knife down at Simeon's feet.

Simeon smiled and bent to pick it up. The knife was wooden, a nearly perfect replica of the knife that now sat tucked behind Tibian's belt.

"I figured a man like you would find a knife beautiful." The king remarked disdainfully. "Now where are my salt and tools?"

Simeon leaned over and whispered to Joseph, who took off for the camp.

"This isn't bad, you did a good job working with the grain of the wood." Simeon turned the wooden blade back and forth in the morning light as he critiqued it.

"Still, there's a lot more to beauty than mere replication. This is good enough for some salt and a bit of dried beef to help out your potatoes. If you want tools, however, you're going to have to put a bit more effort into it."

The king's hand wandered to the handle of his knife as he tried to stare Simeon down, which was hard to do since Simeon wasn't looking at him. The king settled for spitting at Simeon, though he stood too far away to hit him.

"You said if I carved something for you, you would give me salt and tools. I did what you asked, now keep your promise!"

"I told you to make me something beautiful. Tell me, does this look like something your father would have made?"

Simeon's jab hit home and the king's jaw tightened, as did his grip on the handle of his knife. The tension was broken by Joseph returning with a small sack of salt, a handful of dried beef strips, and a new block of wood.

Rather than throw them on the ground, as Simeon would have done, Joseph took the time to walk the items over to the king and hand them to him carefully, making sure none of the beef strips fell into the dirt.

The king gave him a curt nod, then turned and walked back to the house. He hadn't even made it inside the door before he was chewing on one of the beef strips. I can only imagine how wonderful the rich flavor would be to a man who had been eating winter's leftover potatoes.

Tibian made some changes to his routine after that. He made the effort to pull up a new bucket of water and spent a while dipping cupfuls of water and pouring them over his head, sputtering from the coldness of it.

Once the grit and smell of smoke were washed out of his hair, he moved to scrubbing his face as best he could.

Then it was time for his shirt. He washed it as he was wearing it, using a small stone to scrub away at the sturdy fabric. He continued until he was sopping wet and as clean as water without soap could make him.

While waiting to dry, he worked at throwing his knife into the side of the house. It was obviously his first time and more often than not the knife hit flat against the wall with a clang and fell to the ground.

By the time his shirt was dry, he could at least get the blade to stick in point first, though obviously with no pretenses of accuracy.

Then he went to work on his garden. Not wanting to wait for tools from Simeon, he started by walking out a patch by the house that was largely clear of rocks. For hours he worked, pulling weeds and throwing away whatever rocks he found.

Slowly but surely, a patch of dark rich earth grew by the side of the house, large enough to plant his seeds. If the field had been turned over in the fall, the freezing and thawing of the seasons would have loosened the soil enough for him to start planting, even without tools.

As it was, the ground had been neglected too long and the

soil had settled into a hard pack that would take tools to break up.

Having done all he could, the king left and went back inside the house, and we didn't see him the rest of the day.

This ritual repeated itself for several days. A morning bath, throwing his knife, and doing what he could to prepare the ground for his garden. Another week passed before he stood out in the field for another meeting with Simeon.

"You know, I might be able to kill you this morning." The king smiled as he said this and flipped the knife over and over in his hand, spinning it through the air to catch it by the handle each time. "I might not be able to handle your guard dog, but it might be worth it to get you."

Simeon shrugged as if Tibian had been discussing the weather. "It's possible, but you may want to consider if it's worth the loss of your knife, as you wouldn't be getting it back whether you got me or not."

Tibian clutched at his knife possessively. It has been my experience that men who live in solitude, as the king had been doing, tend to form bonds with objects.

For over a week, that knife had been the king's only friend and helper. Suddenly the last thing the king wanted to do was let that knife out of his hand, much less throw it.

"I have carved something." The king switched topics quickly, upset at himself for how badly his attempt at intimidation had gone.

He reached out his hand and a small figure sat in his palm. I noticed that the king did not throw it, as he had the wooden dagger.

From the size alone, I could tell that this had taken a long time to carve down from the original block of wood.

Simeon stepped forward and plucked it out of his hand, stepping well away from the king and his knife before inspecting what he held.

It was a clenched fist. It had been worked into the wood so that the grain looked like veins running along the back of the hand.

Though the skill involved was still a bit raw, the attention to detail was marvelous. Each wrinkle of each knuckle had been carefully scratched into the wood.

The whole thing had been gone over with a stone to sand down any splinters. The surface was as smooth as flesh. He had passed it through a fire, or perhaps just through the smoke, to add dark spots around where one would expect shadows, then scrubbed off any excess.

Even though the wood was lifeless, you could see the strain in the tendons as the hand clenched in some savage emotion.

"This is indeed beautiful." Simeon murmured. "I will give you your tools for this."

"No." The king moved quickly to act on his advantage. "I want tools, a blanket, and a cooking pan."

Simeon studied him for a moment, then his gaze dropped back to the wooden fist. Then he nodded to Joseph.

"Go get him what he asked for."

As Joseph hurried off to gather the objects and another block of wood, Simeon and the king squared off, staring each other down and sizing each other up.

"What is the point of this?" The king finally broke the

silence, true confusion in his voice. "No doubt you feel I wronged you in some way and want to see me suffer for it. I suppose you want me to apologize for something before you kill me, but I can tell you it's not going to happen."

Simeon didn't respond at all and the king fell into a frustrated silence until Joseph returned, his arms brimming with the king's new treasures.

Tibian's eyes immediately went to the blanket, thick and warm. Though the days were warm enough now, the nights were still cold. No doubt a good blanket would mean his first comfortable night since he got there.

Joseph went to hand the items to the king, as he had done before, when Simeon stopped him.

"Lay them on the ground, Joseph, and stand back. We aren't done yet."

The king took an unconscious step back as Simeon took a step forward, advancing on the king.

"What the devil do you mean by this?! What are you doing?"

"I'm going to take your blanket."

"What?" The look on Tibian's face was like a child whose candy had just fallen into the dirt. He immediately snatched the blanket off the ground and clutched it to his chest. "You... We had a deal! I worked my fingers raw carving that fist, I've earned this!"

"A man should be able to defend himself and what he loves." Simeon intoned while still advancing slowly on the king. "You earned that blanket and it is yours, but I am going to take it all the same. Stop me if you can, whelp."

The insult spurred the king to action and he threw the

blanket back onto the ground and snatched the knife from his belt.

He leapt at Simeon, yelling madly, stabbing the knife at Simeon's chest. He moved surprisingly fast, full of the rage that injustice instills in people. But even rage does not trump training.

Simeon twisted, throwing his right arm behind him. The blade meant for Simeon's chest hit empty air and the king stumbled as his momentum carried him forward.

Simeon's left arm snaked over the king's elbow and drew it tight against his body. His right hand came whipping back, slamming into the back of the king's knife hand.

The action would have knocked the arm away, but Simeon held the king's elbow firm, so all the force of the blow forced the king's wrist to bend painfully towards his own forearm.

Simeon kept pushing on the hand and the king gasped from the pain shooting through his arm.

It is simply impossible to maintain a grip on anything when your wrist is in that position, the tendons simply can't shorten far enough.

The knife dropped to the ground from limp fingers. Simeon spun again, in the other direction this time, slamming his palm into Tibian's chest as his left yanked on the king's elbow, throwing him further off balance. He let go of the elbow exactly as the right hand hit.

The effect was the king flying off his feet and landing flat on his back. He made a strange barking noise as he fought for breath.

Simeon strolled over to where the blanket had fallen and threw it over his shoulder. He turned to speak to the king, who had managed to roll to his stomach and push himself up to his knees.

"Asher will see to your instruction. You can train with him as much as you would like. As for me, I will be here every evening with your blanket. When you can take it from me, you can have it."

Once again, Simeon walked away and left his king in the dirt.

Chapter 11

Stories shape the world.

-Musings of the Historian

Tibian suddenly found his days very full indeed. Much of his time was filled tending to his little garden. The ground had to be broken up and worked to create a soft bed for the seeds.

The only water available to him was in the well. The heavy bucket that was more than enough for him proved to be only a sip for the thirsty ground.

Sweat poured from the king's brow as he grunted and strained at the coarse rope. It was his third trip to the well after getting all the seeds planted. He wrestled the bucket from the well as if he were pulling a tree stump from the ground.

He heaved at the handle and half carried, half dragged the bucket over to his garden, sloshing the water down his rows as best he could.

The last bit in the bucket went to the king as he hoisted the bucket above his head and poured the water into his parched mouth, swallowing greedily. The excess splashed over his face and any part of his clothes that weren't already wet.

I had a first row seat to witness this spectacle of honest toil. Simeon had given me permission to go to the house and watch the king for myself.

At first, the king had eyed me with suspicion, yelling at

me to go away. When I continued to hang around, he finally gave up and accepted me as part of the background.

I was sitting on an old stump by the garden as the latest round of water sunk into the ground.

By the look of things, Tibian would need to make at least two more trips to the well to get all of his seeds watered. The despairing look on the king's face told me he had come to the same conclusion.

He turned the bucket over on the ground and sat down on it, exhausted. He turned his attention back to me. His anger was gone. He lifted his hands and showed them to me, palms forward.

His hands were covered in blisters. A couple of the bigger ones had already popped and looked red and angry.

"Do you see that? I never thought I'd see my hands like this. Are most people's hands like this?"

"At first," I responded. "But hands toughen up quickly, then they don't blister anymore."

He looked down at his hands, then back over to the well and decided he wasn't quite ready yet and turned his attention back to me.

"Who are you anyway? You are with these men, but you don't seem like one of them. What role are you supposed to play here? You don't really seem like a killer, and they've already got one of those."

"I'm a storyteller." I find it's best to answer things simply and let people fill in the empty spaces with their own assumptions. The king laughed incredulously at my answer.

"My, my, but they did come prepared, didn't they? If torturing me ever gets boring, they've got a storyteller to entertain them through the slow parts. I'm so happy I at least got the sophisticated kidnappers."

His sarcasm was heavy, but he was too tired and sore to put much force behind it. He ended up sounding genuinely amused.

"Tell me a story, Storyteller. I can offer you a drink of cold water for your services. I'd pay it gladly for something else to think about for a minute."

I smiled. Why not? There's nothing quite like a good story...

"But of course, my king. This has always been one of my favorites...

"There was once an old woodcarver who was known far and wide for his craftsmanship. People traveled far to overpay for his pieces.

"Still, kings and craftsmen all age the same and the time came when his eyes began to dim and his fingers stiffened.

"He had made plenty of money and he had more than enough to support himself and his family.

"And yet he worried about his son, who had been supported by the father's labors his whole life. He was afraid that his boy would never know the joy the woodcarver had gained from his trade.

"So one day as he sat by the fire, he called his son into him and told him to carve him something. That way, he could die happy knowing that his son had shared in his craft.

"The young man had no interest in spending that kind of time in his father's drafty woodworking shed, but he was a good son and wanted his father to be happy.

94

"So he went into town and chose a lovely carved wooden bird he thought his father would enjoy. He bought it and brought it back to his father, proudly proclaiming it to be his own work.

"Without saying a word, the old woodcarver threw the bird into the fire. The son hurried from his father's presence, angry at himself for being such a fool.

"Certainly his father would know that he wasn't capable of such fine work, not yet. He went back into town the next day and found a carver's apprentice who was idly working on a figure of a wolf.

"The young man immediately bought the rough looking wolf from the lad, refusing to hear the boy's protests that it wasn't worth it and barely looked like a wolf at all.

"He hurried back to his father, pausing only to pull a splinter out of his hand from the unfinished wolf figure. Once again, he presented the carving to his father, apologizing for the rough work and his previous deception.

"Once again, the father threw the carving into the fire without a single word.

"The son wandered from the room in a stupor. He felt ashamed for trying to fool his father. Finally finding his integrity, he rushed to the workshop and worked furiously for two days, carving the figure of a boat.

"When it was done, it was a far cry from anything he could sell at market, but it was his own. He wrapped his blistered and splintered fingers around it like a prayer and carried it into his father.

"He approached his father reverently and laid the boat on his lap. 'Father, I have carved this for you,' the son whispered.

"Without a word, his father grabbed the boat and threw it into the fire.

"Horrified, the young man leapt to the fire and thrust his hand in, snatching his boat back from the hungry flames. He turned back to his father to see that a broad and contented smile now warmed the old man's face.

"'Now that one, you carved.' The father said."

I fell silent as the story ended. The king continued to stare at me as if expecting me to continue. It was a while before he spoke.

"You tell strange stories. Most of my storytellers tell me tales of great battles and my father's prowess in war. What kind of story was that?"

"That was a story about you, my king."

"You know, I haven't quite made up my mind, but there is a good possibility that you are insane." He shook his head and chuckled, rising to his feet and dusting off his bucket. "Here, let me pull you a drink."

I enjoyed a long cold drink from the next bucketful before Tibian lugged it over to the garden.

As soon as the king had managed to get water to all his rows, Asher was there for training. Tibian objected weakly, showing off the blisters on his hands.

He must have been exhausted indeed to think that he would get pity from a man like Asher. The dark-eyed man slapped the blistered hands down as the king grimaced in pain.

Asher set to his task immediately, molding the young king into the shape he wanted. He kicked at his feet until they were just over shoulder width apart.

A few taps with the toe of his boot got Tibian's knees bent to the angle Asher wanted. His back was straightened, his arms raised and his torso turned.

"Why did you lose your fight last night?" The old soldier asked. The king started to straighten up and drop his hands and Asher hit him, hard, across the face with his palm.

Coming from another person, it might have looked like a slap. Coming from Asher it was a powerful strike with a blunt object.

Tibian staggered and almost fell, his hand up at his face. Asher stalked after him, raising his hand as if to strike again.

"You can't stop my hand if you're coddling your cheek. Get back into the stance I showed you and do not move from it until I tell you."

If it had been Simeon, the king might have been inspired to glare or talk back, but this was Asher, and Gholost inspired only fear.

The king hurried back into his stance, adjusting his feet a couple times as he tried to remember exactly where Asher had put them.

"I ask you again, why did you lose your fight against Simeon?"

"He surprised me." The king spoke through his raised arms, not daring to lower them. Asher snorted scornfully.

"He announced he was attacking and advanced on you slowly. You struck first and were armed. I have never had an enemy so concerned for my welfare."

The king flustered, but he didn't dare break stance while Asher was within striking distance.

"You're supposed to be the teacher. Why don't you just tell me?" The king was angry, but he worked hard at making his tone respectful. It sounded a bit like a man talking soothingly to a growling dog.

"Since you are just a pup of a man, I will. You lost because you fell down. As long as you're on your feet, you have limitless options.

"You can advance, retreat, sidestep, feint, attack, defend, jump, roll, or any number of quick maneuvers to place your enemy where you want him.

"As soon as you've lost your feet, your options plummet and so do your chances for survival.

"If Simeon had wanted to last night, he could have taken your knife and plunged it into your chest, or put his boots to you and broken your ribs.

"It is the least of what I would have done. The stance I have taught you will be how you stand whenever you are in a fight. If you ever move out of that stance, you will fall on your royal butt and die like a dog in the dirt."

Tibian nodded numbly, raising his hands a little higher. Asher circled around him like a shark, studying his form. When he again stood in front of him, he pushed gently on Tibian's chest.

Tibian was suddenly off balance, back on his heels. If Asher had wanted to, he could have pushed him down with a flick of his wrist. Instead he let the king reset and adjust before he did it again.

This time Tibian was ready, having shifted his weight over his toes and bending his knees more. Asher grunted approval.

He continued his inspection, giving little pushes here and

there and letting the king fine tune his stance. It was infinitely more effective than trying to explain all of the subtleties of balance. He let the king learn it himself. When he was satisfied, he stood back again and spoke.

"Remember how you are in this moment. This is your stance, your space. While you maintain this stance, no one can knock you down and kill you. How does it feel?"

"Honestly, my legs are burning and my arms are tired after my day's work. I think I got it, can I stand back up now?" The king's knees betrayed the truth of the matter as they shook ever so slightly. Asher shook his head firmly.

"Your muscles are loose and weak. Your body and mind have softened without hardship. If you ever hope to be anything but a spoiled whelp, you will command your body to obey your mind, for that is where the soul resides."

Rather deep words from a ruthless killer, I reflected. Asher continued.

"You are like a baby taking his first step. You have managed to get yourself into a decent stance once, with help, and while standing still.

"With a little luck, you might be able to bungle your way back into one later on your own.

"This stance must become your new normal. You must practice it until it is as natural and comfortable as sitting down. It should be how you rise from your bed in the morning. It should be how you carry your bucket.

"You should be able to move around quickly without shifting from your stance. When you can do this, you will be ready to claim your blanket."

This was too much for the king and he protested.

"Look, I understand that I need to keep my balance in a fight, but this is just a stance. When do I learn how to punch or kick and strike down my opponent? Fighting is far more than learning how to stand around."

"A demonstration, then?" Asher's tone was helpful and patient, but my trained ear could detect the underlying impatience. This wasn't likely to end well for the king.

"You go ahead and stand back up and attack me. You can use whatever you'd like, punch and kick to your heart's content. I will not raise a finger to strike you back. I will simply... stand around."

Tibian straightened up with a sigh of relief, flexing his sore legs. Thinking to be sneaky, he struck out quickly and without preamble, throwing a fist at Asher's face throwing his whole body weight behind the blow.

It was a classic bar room cheap shot and it might have worked on someone slow and drunk. As it was, Asher stepped quickly, not away from the strike, but into it. The king's fist hit empty air where Asher's face used to be.

His forward momentum carried his chest right into Asher's shoulder, which was suddenly very close.

It was like a bird smacking into a window. The king was mid-leap, fully extended. Asher was set low, his feet planted solid on the ground. Tibian bounced comically off Asher and fell hard to the dirt.

He sprang up quickly, his bruised pride taking priority over his sore legs. He approached Asher more carefully this time, moving slowly. He walked in swinging heavy rights and lefts, each one going for a knockout.

Asher kept shifting away out of reach. Finally, frustrated at hitting air, the king threw his leg out in an extended kick, hoping to catch Asher at his next step back.

The problem was, Asher didn't step back. He stepped forward, moving like a flicker at the corner of your eye. The king's foot hit against Asher's hip, but far too early in its stomping motion, so there was almost no striking force.

Instead, the pushing motion meant to knock Asher back pushed the king off balance and he stumbled backwards.

Asher danced forward, giving his opponent no chance to set himself. Another bump was all it took and Tibian landed in the dirt once again.

This time he hit hard enough to knock the breath out of him. As he caught his breath again, he took the time to look up at Asher standing over him.

In a short scuffle, Asher had managed to knock the king around like a rag doll and he wasn't even breathing heavily.

"Would you like me to explain any further?"

The king shook his head, still catching his breath. When he could stand again, Asher drilled the newly humbled monarch endlessly on how to stand.

He had him come off the ground into the stance from every conceivable position. Asher would check how well the king had remembered his lesson by shoving him from time to time.

If the king was in a good stance, he was able to resist or regain his balance almost instantly. If not, he ended up sprawled on the ground again.

As promised, when the evening came, Simeon came out

with the blanket and stood waiting for the king's challenge.

It never came. Tibian was so tired from the day's training he could barely walk, much less fight a seasoned soldier. On the bright side, I doubted he had any trouble falling asleep that night, blanket or no.

Chapter 12

Plans crumble. Pay close attention to what remains when they do.

-Musings of the Historian

That is how the days passed for the next two weeks. Tibian worked himself doggedly. In the cold morning hours, he would crouch around the fire carving some new trinket to trade for more beef or other necessities. I couldn't help but smile when the next piece he presented to Simeon was a boat, a squat river craft.

When his carving was done, he went to work on watering his garden, which was still a tremendous affair, though his blisters faded, replaced by rough calluses. At times, Joseph would help him.

With the two of them working together, they had time afterward for Joseph to show the king how to mend his roof so he wouldn't get wet at the next rain.

Tibian got along quite well with Joseph, and the two could often be seen talking and laughing as they worked on some new project. These tasks usually had something to do with making the house more livable.

The king even got to the point where his combat lessons went smoothly as the young monarch rushed to obey Asher's commands.

Tibian proved to be a promising student, and though I knew he would never show it, I knew Asher was pleased.

Tibian started challenging Simeon for the blanket every night. He wasn't close to taking the blanket from him yet, but he would swell with pleasure each time he managed to sidestep an attack or get Simeon a little off balance.

Once, he even landed a punch full on Simeon's face. He lost worse than usual that night. He went back to his house with a swollen eye and bleeding lip. The following day, however, he whistled as he went about his chores.

As the king had got to know the other members of the party, his hate and frustration gathered together. It focused in intensity like a sunbeam through a magnifying glass. All of it now fell on Simeon.

He had approached each of us in turn, asking us to help him escape, to sneak him things, or anything to make his life easier. One by one we turned him down.

All of us had signed on with Simeon, each for their own reasons. None of us would break that trust until this charade was done. When he met with these refusals, the king didn't blame us; he blamed Simeon.

In many ways, the tall quiet man had become the embodiment of everything evil for the king. He saved all of his anger and frustration for their nightly fights.

He seemed more than willing to endure harm if it meant a chance to get back at Simeon somehow.

Frankly, I worried at times that this fascinating experiment would end early if Simeon ever dropped his guard long enough for Tibian to plant his dagger in his back.

I didn't doubt that Tibian would do it if given the chance. His hand always seemed to stray to the knife at his belt every time Simeon was near.

By the end of the two weeks, Tibian was able to make a good showing of himself in the nightly fights. Already his movements were starting to look like Asher's as he emulated his teacher.

After getting beaten at the end of the two weeks, Tibian announced that he had a row of carrots sprouting up, as well as a row of peas.

To hear the pride and grandeur in his voice, you would think he had announced the victorious conclusion of a war. Simeon nodded calmly and turned to Joseph.

"We're out of a lot of things ourselves. Would you go into town and pick us up some supplies? And do get some carrots and peas for our majesty here."

"Of course, I'll leave later tonight and be there as soon as the markets open." Joseph couldn't keep the pleasure from his voice any more than the king.

Though he was bleeding from a split lip, the king gave a regal smile to Joseph, a condescending scowl to Simeon, and turned and strode back to his house like he was entering a castle.

I remember thinking what a good night that was. By trickery and against his will, Tibian was learning to be a man. He had worked first for survival, as all people will when pressed. But there was a steel in him now that hadn't been there before.

His transformation was physical as well. His shoulders were growing broad and strong lugging the heavy water bucket back and forth to and from the garden.

His fat was melting away under the heat of the hard work and simple food. His face, which I had described as round before, had sprouted high cheekbones and a square jaw which had been hidden away beneath his softer layers.

Even the way he walked was different. You would think that a king would walk with confidence, but it is easy to see the difference between the spoiled stomping of a soft aristocrat and the smooth stride of a man who knows that he is capable of whatever needs to be done.

A good night indeed, but it couldn't last.

The next morning, everything changed.

I had found myself a good spot, isolated from the camp, where I could see the camp and the house equally well.

Asher was by the fire, sharpening some kind of hook. It had strange fittings on it and looked like it strapped onto his arm.

I wondered idly if it was the kind of hook he used climbing the castle wall. A clever man could use such a thing to find holds that mere fingers couldn't cling to.

Simeon was a distance from the camp, walking the tree line, stretching his legs as he watched the king. Tibian had successfully waited out the morning chill, carving by his own fire. Now he was washing himself off at the well as best he could before he started his strenuous watering routine.

Technically, his deal with Simeon got him food just for getting them to sprout, but he seemed intent on following through with it for his own reasons. I have heard that gardens are like that.

Sudden motion caught my eye and I saw Joseph scrambling through the woods, heedless of the branches that tore at his clothes and face. Instinctively I looked behind him to see who or what was chasing him, but there was nothing.

As soon as he got close enough, he spotted Simeon and changed his course to tear after him. Simeon heard the footsteps and spun to meet his brother.

He must have made the same assumption I had because his hand went immediately to his sword and he shifted to his right to look behind his running brother for pursuers.

Joseph stumbled before he got to Simeon and his brother jumped forward to catch him before he lost his balance entirely. As soon as he had hold of him he held his little brother out at arm's length, searching him frantically for wounds.

Joseph brushed the hands away and grabbed his brother in an embrace, clutching at him as he spoke into his ear between gasping breaths.

I cursed myself for being so far away. Joseph was no coward, but even from hundreds of paces away, he looked like a man broken.

Whatever his mental affliction was, it passed with full force to Simeon. He sank to his knees and Joseph was left standing over him. Simeon clutched at his head like a man in pain.

I don't remember rising from my seat, but the next thing I knew I was running across the field as fast as I could without raising suspicion. I needed to know what was going on.

Out of the corner of my eye, I saw Asher doing the same. Joseph's rampage through the woods must have drawn his attention away from his tools. He was rushing to Simeon as quickly as I was.

We reached him at the same time, taking a moment to

trade worried glances with each other. Simeon would not look up, he was completely lost in his own personal agony.

We looked to Joseph for an explanation, but he just shook his head, not up for regular communication after his journey through the forest and whatever trauma had prompted it.

When Simeon raised his head, it was to look past my right shoulder. I turned to see Tibian standing there, looking as confused as the rest of us.

Tears streamed down Simeon's cheeks and he waved the king forward wordlessly. Tibian obeyed meekly, stunned as the rest of us were at this sudden breakdown. Even Asher looked unsettled.

"Your majesty," the sarcasm and taunts were gone, Simeon spoke with deep sincerity, his voice breaking with emotion. "You are free to go.

"You may take anything you like from our camp and go where you will. You are welcome to stay here if you'd like, it might be best if you did."

"Why? What are you talking about? What kind of trick is this?" Panic laced Tibian's voice as he tried to make sense of the scene unfolding before him. Simeon had to take several deep breaths before he could speak.

"The Marauders have taken the capitol, the nation belongs to them. Joseph tells me the few factions of the Land Guard that stood up to them were swept aside. They are organized now, a true conquering army. They hold everything."

The king looked desperately to Joseph, hoping for some hint that it was all a trick. Joseph could only nod through his own grief. He looked back to Simeon.

"What can I do?"

"Nothing. Absolutely nothing."

"But... but I am the king."

"You are king of nothing!" Simeon was suddenly on his feet and right in the king's face. Rage and frustration boiled to the surface as the truth sank in. Everything he had dedicated his life to was gone, lost into darkness on a sunny morning.

"You are nothing but a spoiled brat of a boy who isn't worthy of his father's blood! This is your fault!

"You weakened our country through your selfishness and neglect. You made us a ripe peach for the plucking!"

"Well if you hadn't taken me away..." The king defended himself feebly.

"If we hadn't taken you away, you'd be dead right now! You'd be tortured and displayed on a spike for all the people to see. We..." Simeon started, but thought better of it.

"I kidnapped you so that maybe this disaster could be averted. I stole you from that castle thinking I could turn you into a man worthy of leading this nation. But I was a fool. I am a fool and you're a dead man if they ever find you."

Simeon spat the last words out like they were venom in his mouth. It took the last of his anger with it and his shoulders slumped again, weary with defeat and despair.

He turned and waved his hand at the king, dismissing him from his mind and his plans with a flick of his wrist.

We all stood and watched him as he trudged back to the campfire and planted himself on a log in front of it. He stared into the dwindling flames of the morning cook fire. The rest of us were left standing around in silence. It was Tibian who finally spoke.

"What did he mean? That part about why you kidnapped me."

"The country was weak." Joseph had found his voice again, though he spoke as if to himself. "You taxed everyone out of their hopes and left everything to waste away.

"While everybody else set to taking what they could or scheming against you, Simeon had a plan to show you what it meant to live as a common man in your kingdom. He thought it might give you strength."

In any other situation, the words would have brought on an onslaught of sarcasm from the king. As it was, there didn't seem to be anything to say. All arguments had become meaningless.

After a few minutes of standing in awkward silence, our little group split up and went their separate ways. I found myself in a full blown quandary.

Joseph naturally went after his brother, which I had expected. The king retreated to his house, which was also expected. What wasn't expected was that Asher followed along after Tibian. I found myself pulled in three directions.

In one direction, I had the brothers who had started this whole thing, Simeon the mastermind and Joseph with the loyal heart.

In another lay the once-king, dethroned while he sat in the dirt; and the dark assassin called Hunger.

In the third direction lay the distant mountains and the horizon that held a strong pull that I could never fight for long without a story to witness.

There was a part of me that felt the story was over. It had

a lot of potential, but in the end, the timing just didn't pan out.

So I found myself standing out in the field, mere feet from where Simeon had knelt in his despair. I felt rooted to the spot, tied down as if by three ropes.

Any time I decided to go one way, the possibilities of the other two pulled my mind immediately back to center. I don't know how long I stood there. As I've said before, time is a fuzzy subject for one like myself.

It was Simeon who finally interrupted my reverie.

"Our story has ended, Storyteller." His eyes were red and puffy from crying. His shoulders slumped and his head nodded ever so slightly, as if it took all his strength to stand erect.

"I asked you along as an impartial judge. I ask you now to fulfill your debt. Judge me, traveler. I would hear the truth from you, even if it be my condemnation."

"You are a fool, Simeon." I pronounced. He rocked a bit, as if my words had been fists. Still he nodded, though his eyes filled with tears as he did it.

"You are first a fool to believe that there could ever be an impartial judge. Our perception of reality is shaped by our experiences and our choices. Every mortal experience is unique.

"You are twice a fool to believe this story is over. I cannot believe that the four men here will simply fade into darkness.

"And you are lastly a fool if you think I would pass judgment until the story is done."

I realized in that moment that I had made up my own mind. The story wasn't over yet. If anything, it had only started to build toward a crescendo. I would stay and watch. As the decision was made, I felt the urge to walk on fade into the background.

It was never truly gone.

Impulsively I reached out and clapped Simeon on the shoulder. Then I turned and walked to the house where Tibian and Asher sat within. Casting a glance back before I entered, I saw Simeon right where I had left him, his head hung low.

Chapter 13

Everything changes with perspective.

–Musings of the Historian

The day still had surprises in store for me as I walked into the house. Asher immediately threw me against a wall and held a knife to my throat. The look in his eyes wasn't angry or bloodthirsty, merely calculating.

"Listen, Storyteller, Simeon trusted you and I trusted Simeon; but everything has changed now and I'd like to know some things for myself. Why don't we start with your name?"

"I don't have one." My simple and honest answer caused a flare of anger in Asher and the knife pressed a little harder against my throat.

"Don't try to play games, Storyteller. Look at my eyes and ask yourself if I would hesitate to slit you wide open. Again, what is your name?"

"I spoke the truth, Asher. Perhaps you should look at my eyes and ask yourself if you see any deception... or fear."

Asher's expression turned puzzled as he searched my face. This was an old tactic of mine in tense situations.

Generally, people pay very little attention to me anyway. Some deep instinct keeps them from looking too closely. But inevitably someone like Asher would disregard those inner urges and get right up in my face. That's when they felt it.

There's something about me that simply doesn't fit. I can't feel it myself, but when people look at me, I can see it in their eyes. It's a bit like looking at a room you left a moment ago and having all the furniture moved exactly half an inch.

Nothing can really explain it and there's nothing quite wrong; it just doesn't add up. I saw this confusion in Asher's face as his mind tried to place me in a comfortable category. It wouldn't work.

Still, there was a risk that someone like Asher would choose to slit my throat on the basis of not understanding me. That would cause a lot more uncomfortable questions and I would have to leave.

I can count on one hand the number of times I've been able to stay after an event like that, it's too much for people. In any event, I thought it best to move to distract Asher while he was still feeling the confusion.

"I think a better question is why you are here, Asher. You spoke of your great debt to Ander, and yet as soon as things crumbled, you have followed the king. Why? Would you have us believe you are actually a patriot?"

"I don't think it's your place to examine my motives, Storyteller." His tone was angry, but the knife had crept away from my neck, now resting on my chest. "Why are you here? I thought you were a friend of Simeon's."

"He asked me along to witness what he planned to do. Now that he feels it's over, he doesn't really need me anymore, does he?"

"We don't need you here either. I've never been fond of witnesses myself."

"He can stay." Tibian finally joined the conversation, speaking over his shoulder from his seat by the fire. "I doubt his sanity, but I can't believe he'd be any harm either."

"Yes, your majesty." Asher's tone was subservient as he lowered his knife and stepped back. I shot him an incredulous look. I couldn't believe Asher bowing before any man.

With his back to the king, the look he flashed back at me was vicious and threatening, warning me not to say anything. Asher had his own game going here and he was making it clear from the start that he would not look kindly on any interference.

It looked like I had chosen the right camp. There was already intrigue building here and all I had done was walk through the door.

"So what are you going to do?" Patience is a funny thing. Normally I was more than content to sit by and watch a story unfold. But I couldn't help feeling that things were happening fast outside this peaceful clearing.

If the king was going to do much of anything, it would need to happen soon.

"I am going to take my kingdom back." The king stated forcefully. It was the answer I was hoping for, though it was a bit selfish of me.

A simple life in exile would likely be a safer choice for the king, but what a boring story that would make.

"And how will you be going about that?" I nudged. I suspected I knew the answer to this question as well.

"I have no idea." Tibian didn't disappoint. Still, it wasn't said as an indication of despair. Rather he seemed to be taking it as his first obstacle. "Obviously I need to get the Land Guard together under my command."

Even with his new act of willing servant, Asher was unable to suppress a snort at the idea. Tibian raised a questioning eyebrow at him, but turned to me for an explanation.

"You must be careful, your majesty, not to express a problem in terms of a solution, it limits the mind."

Tibian's look only grew more confused. I pressed on. "You need to look at the actual problem, not just what you think needs to be done.

"For example, if I had just bought a piece of leather and I wanted it in strips, I could say, 'I need a knife.' But that just shuts down my mind to other solutions. So instead of trading the piece for leather strips, or getting someone else to cut it for me, I spend all my time looking around for a knife I don't have."

"I do see some sense in what you're saying, Storyteller, but I still don't see what it has to do with my gaining control of the Land Guard."

"Because it's a bloody waste of time!" Asher had grown tired of my instructive approach and jumped in on the conversation.

"If the Land Guard were strong enough to throw the Marauders out, they would have stopped them in the first place while they still had a defensive advantage.

"Even if they were strong enough, almost none of the commanders know you at all. Any nobility or officers who were loyal enough to stand by you were likely in that castle when it was taken. Any sort of pull you might have had with the Guard is dead, and I do mean dead."

Tibian had started looking a bit sick. I'm sure he wanted to be angry with Asher for his harsh words, but it was hard when everything hit so close to home. He wouldn't even have a name to call if he wanted to talk with somebody from his disbanded army.

"Umm, you were saying something, Storyteller. Perhaps you would like to explain a little more?" His first whisper of a plan had been shot down like a cream puff in front of a cannon. It didn't take much for a man in that position to start grasping at straws.

"All I'm saying is that you need to take a step back and try to look at your problem clearly. Now, what is your problem?"

"I don't have an army." His voice was still a bit subdued from Asher's tirade.

"No, that's not your problem."

"I don't have support from my own people?"

"I'd say that is a problem, but you're still not there yet."

"My land has a bunch of Marauders in it!" The king threw his hands in the air, exasperated.

"There you go," I smiled brightly like a proud teacher. The king was less than impressed.

"Well gee, thanks for helping me get to that. I knew I was overlooking something." Sarcasm dripped from his voice and he mumbled something that sounded a bit like "crazy vagrant."

I could hardly deny the charge, but I wasn't about to let my brilliant lesson go to waste either.

"And now you see the real problem, what are your possible solutions?" It was proof of how low the king had fallen that he allowed me to baby-step him through his own thoughts.

"I can kill them all or I can force them to run, though I don't know how I'm supposed to do that without an army."

"I couldn't agree more, my king. Asher," I looked towards the dark figure behind the king. "Can you think of any options our monarch has overlooked?"

"We can make them want to leave on their own." It was a perfect answer from a man who wore fear like a warm coat.

Tibian was suddenly hopeful, grabbing at the hem of Asher's sleeve as he looked up at him.

"Could you do it? Can you make them afraid enough that they leave?"

I smiled at the king's childlike innocence and naiveté. Asher shook his head.

"No, my king. You can't drive out an occupying force with a single guerrilla fighter. I am a warrior without equal," Asher said this in a way that made it a statement of fact, not boasting, "but I am limited to what I see before me. You need someone who can plan a war, not a battle."

"So what then?" More despair was creeping into Tibian's voice as his situation became clearer and clearer.

"You need Simeon."

"What?!" Tibian's despair was gone in a flash, replaced with burning anger. "You expect me to ask him for help after what he did to me? You're as crazy as this addle-brained wanderer."

"I was the one who took you from the castle, your majesty. Why are you accepting help from me?"

"It's different, you were doing what he told you to. The way he talked to me, no one has ever... I can't believe he would be so..." The king's face turned red as he floundered for words.

Simeon had been the focal point for all his rage and

118

feelings of helplessness for too long. Even now that the world had turned upside down for him, all he could remember was Simeon's face looming over him in his deepest moments of shame.

"I would rather die than accept help from that pompous speck of a man!" The king rallied his emotions and let them all out, yelling his final ultimatum.

"As a man, that is your prerogative." It was time for me to push him one last time. "As a king, it's a bit more complicated than that. So you must choose if you are a man or a king."

"You know, I'm getting tired of your riddles. What are you talking about, man or king?"

"Try this, my king. Let me tell you a story, and you tell me how it ends. A man falls on hard times and while walking along the street, a rival of his laughs at his ratty clothes and tosses a loaf of bread at the man's feet. Tell me, should the man pick it up?"

"Never!" Tibian spoke through clenched teeth, his emotions high.

"Well spoken, my king. His pride should never bend for such a trifle. But what if the man were a father, with a wife and children at home who had not seen bread in days?"

Tibian opened his mouth to speak, then stopped himself, realizing the trap into which he had fallen.

"I suppose he should probably pick up the bread." The king spoke in a mumble, confessing the truth against his will.

"Right you are, my king, how wise of you not to let the man's pride be a harm to those that depend on him.

"Now let me take this one step further. What if the man had thousands of children at home?"

"What?" The king scoffed and smiled at the ridiculous

image. "That would be ludicrous. No man has thousands of children."

"I may be a crazy vagabond, my king, but stay with me for a moment more. If the man had thousands of children at home, would it not be the right thing for the man to pick up the bread, thank the man for his generosity, and ask him for more?"

"I suppose," The king still chuckled at the absurd situation. "If a man found himself in such a position, he would have to do everything in his power to try and feed his thousands of children. By that time, he wouldn't have much of a choice."

"And what is a king but the father of a nation?" The king's smile vanished from his face as if it had shattered. "Your pride is your own, your majesty, but at some point you must make a simple decision, one that will define your whole life."

"And what decision is that?"

"Are you a man, are you a father, or are you a king?"

Tibian's jaw hung slack as my trap swung closed. I had put him into a corner with only one way out. Really, he had been there the whole time. I had merely shed light on his situation.

"Curse you, Storyteller." Tibian whispered.

Chapter 14

The weight of history swings on choices. To understand why people make the choices they do is to understand the whole of history and most of the future.

-Musings of the Historian

We set off to look for Simeon and Joseph early the next morning, hoping to find them at the camp. Luck wasn't with us, however. The camp was cleared out.

Piles of provisions had been set out for the king, but the tents and other gear were gone, along with Simeon and Joseph.

The king took a moment to walk to one pile in particular. The blanket that had been taken from him sat on the top of the pile. Tibian ran his fingers over the soft cloth, the look on his face almost reverent.

He lifted it gently and pressed it to the side of his face, his eyes closed. Some troubling thought invaded his moment, however, and his face grew angry again. He set the blanket down again and turned to Asher.

"We still need them. Can you track them to wherever they went?"

"Of course." Asher knelt and pressed his fingers into the dark ashes where the fire used to be. "This fire has been out for more than just the night. The fire heats the ground underneath and the ashes form a blanket that keeps it warm long after the fire is gone.

"This ground is cold. My guess is they packed up while our story-telling friend stood out in the field and left as soon as he and Simeon had their little talk. Did he say anything to you about where they might go?"

I shook my head, Asher shrugged.

"It doesn't matter much, there's only a couple of options open to them. We just need to figure out what they've chosen."

"Can't you just follow their tracks?" The king had started pacing impatiently. "We're wasting time."

"We would waste more time if we went barging off into the forest without thinking first, my king. Sure, I can follow their tracks, the marks men make on the wilderness as they pass. But that takes time, hunting for shadows over rocks and soft leaves.

"They won't be looking at the ground, they'll be moving as quickly as they can and they've got a great head start.

"Our only hope of catching them is to track them first using our minds, then we can hurry to catch up to them."

"Oh... all right." The king spoke sheepishly, having once again taken an education in patience. "What do you mean they only have a couple of options? They could have gone anywhere."

Asher shook his head again.

"A wild creature only runs towards water, food, or away from a predator. Men are much the same.

"Simeon can only return to what he knows, try to help in some way; or he can choose to leave the country altogether, start anew in some new land."

"Do you think Simeon would leave?" The king asked, careful now not to make assumptions.

"No, I don't. That means that he will likely return to his father's house, gather supplies, and leave from there. After that, he'll either disappear or get himself killed, depending on how his mind is working. In any event, we need to catch him before he leaves the house.

"At least we know he'll waste a little time there trying to talk Joseph out of coming with him. That gives us some time to catch up. Gather all the supplies you can carry easily, give priority to water containers. We'll need to move fast."

All three of us pitched in and gathered what we could, filling our pockets with dried fruits and meats, wrapping blankets around ourselves like sashes.

By the time we were ready to move out, we looked more like traveling peddlers than a king and his retinue.

Asher led, setting a grueling pace. The king's feet managed to find every raised root and hidden rock. More than once Asher looked over his shoulder to scowl at the king as he stumbled his way through the wood. I also tripped once, but it was just to make the king feel better.

By my best calculation, we were about four hours away from the brothers' home at the pace Asher set. As long as we didn't stop for breaks or rests, we would make it there by afternoon easily.

Of course, I couldn't count on that. After the first hour, the king was already puffing and limping, having twisted his ankle on his latest fall.

I had to give him credit for the effort he was making, but he wasn't in the physical shape necessary for a forced march. The upper body strength he had gained with his training and his water bucket didn't help him much now.

We finally paused for a rest after the king started having trouble rising after he tripped. Asher paced, an ironic way to rest from a long march.

He would glance first south, to where the brothers' house lay somewhere in the distance, then back to the miserable king, who was rubbing at his stiff ankle and blistered feet.

His hands had become tough and hardened from his enforced farm work, but his feet were still the soft feet of a noble.

Though I felt sorry for him, I probably had more in common with Asher at that moment. It was infuriating to wait when it may already be too late. There was no telling how long the brothers would wait at the house.

Chances were Simeon would take off again as soon as he was able. Once he was gone, it would be virtually impossible to find him. Knowing Simeon, he'd be taking pains to avoid being found.

"You know..." I started, sidling over to where Asher scowled at the sun. "I could go on ahead and try to catch Simeon and Joseph before they leave the house. I could move much faster on my own."

The look Asher shot me would have burned holes through iron. I suspect part of his frustration was not thinking of it first. I'm sure if he had his way, he would leave the king with me and be running through the woods.

Still, he didn't trust me. While that made him hesitant to let me go off on my own, it was much worse considering leaving me alone with the king.

In the end, he nodded, though anyone could tell he didn't

like it. He simply didn't have much choice.

I matched the pace Asher had set until I was out of sight of the two men, then I really stretched out my legs and started eating up the distance. Trees brushed by as I wove my way through the forest in full swing.

At one point I burst into a clearing and startled a small herd of deer who froze solid for a moment before bounding away, terrified at the strange man who came out of nowhere and shot at them like a hawk.

Moving at my own pace, it wasn't long before I found the sturdy stone house. I breathed a sigh of relief as I heard sounds coming from within. It seemed I wasn't too late after all.

My euphoria was short-lived, however, as I entered the house to find Joseph, alone. He was packing frantically and swearing furiously under his breath.

He didn't even notice when I walked in the door and almost ran into me as he turned suddenly to grab something from the bed.

He was less than happy to see me.

"What the devil do you want? I thought you went off with the king and Asher. Fat lot of good any of you were, anyway."

"Joseph, where is Simeon?" I asked tentatively, though I already knew the answer.

"Gone! The sad piece of dung picked up and left. He said he'd take first watch and start packing while I took a nap after our walk here.

"I woke up half an hour ago, the sun high in the sky and he's gone. The next time I see him I'm going to knock his teeth out and wear them like a necklace."

I couldn't help but smile as the kindhearted Joseph ranted and raved about the violence he intended for his brother. It was so out of character to see him swearing like a sailor. Being left behind had filled him with impotent rage.

Still, I was more than a little worried about what all this meant. Obviously Simeon had left his brother behind to protect him.

That could only mean that he meant to do something really dangerous that he didn't want his brother to be a part of.

Since he hadn't flinched at including his brother in kidnapping the king, I could only assume that what he intended next would border on insanity.

"So are you going after him?"

"Of course I'm bloody going after him, you half-brained twit! He's my brother, what's he going to do without me? Get himself killed, that's what."

Joseph's voice broke just a little at that last statement, betraying the river of emotion flowing underneath his anger. I guessed he had come to the same conclusion I had.

He shouldered his pack and deliberately shoved by me, though I was hardly in his way. I scrambled to follow him out the door.

"Now wait a minute, Joseph. Asher and the king are coming here, we were coming to ask Simeon for help. We need him. Why don't you wait for them and we can go looking for him together?"

"Forget it, traveler." Joseph started walking faster, trying to get away from me. "I've lost too much time already. I'm not taking the word of a half mad wanderer to wait around for a fallen king and a mad dog."

"Well at least tell me where we can find you. Joseph, you have to give the king a chance to take his kingdom back."

This stopped him short and he turned to stare at me.

"You know, I take back the part about you being half mad. You are completely mad, full-gone nuts!

"I don't know if you heard the details, but the war already happened and we lost. We lost everything. All I've got left is my brother and I don't even have that.

"I'll tell you what, traveler, every week I'll check the lists at the graveyards for your name. Oh wait, you never told me your name, so I guess this is goodbye."

He turned and walked off, waving his hand behind him in a mix of farewell and dismissal. Once he disappeared down the trail I was left alone again with my thoughts.

This story was starting to stretch thin. If much more went wrong, the whole thing would spiral into tragedy. Somehow the players needed to come back together.

Now, one might think it was foolish of me to pin so much hope on the actions of a few people, especially where armies had failed. But I am, above all things, the Historian. And any historian knows that the wheels of history don't turn on the acts of armies and populations. It is the acts of individuals that change the world.

It is an insane delusion I have noticed in people. They stop themselves from trying to accomplish great things with the rationalization that their contributions are too small to make any difference against the vastness of the world's problems.

Yet every history book they crack open is an endless list of individuals, often starting from nothing, who decided one day they didn't like the way things were.

So these individuals set out to change the world, and before anyone sensible explained to them how foolish they were being, they had done it.

This is what I hoped to see in this story. If anything, four people seemed like plenty.

I was tempted to follow after Joseph, he likely had the best chance of finding Simeon. In the end, I decided against it. I was already participating in this story more than usual. I had made my decision to stay with Asher and Tibian and I would stick with it for now.

It must have only gotten rougher for them, because the sun was already sitting low on the mountains by the time Asher walked out of the woods.

The king limped out almost a full minute later, limping so badly it looked as if he was dragging one foot behind him.

It was an especially bad sign that the leg he was favoring wasn't the one he had twisted the ankle on earlier. Something had happened that made his strong foot even worse than his twisted one.

Asher looked to me for a verdict. I shook my head slightly and he swore bitterly under his breath. By the time Tibian made his way to me, Asher was already rummaging around inside the stone house, working on a fire for the evening.

"They're gone, aren't they?" The defeat in Tibian's voice was total. I sized him up as he stood before me. I don't know how it might have happened, but he had lost a shoe. One of his feet was wrapped in a white strip torn from his shirt. Blood showed through the edges of the cloth where it had seeped out to the sides.

His whole body screamed exhaustion. Even as he spoke to me, he swayed a little, as if the light breeze passing through the clearing would be enough to knock him over. I couldn't help but admire him a bit in that moment.

His will alone had carried him so fast and so far with his feet injured. The distance wasn't that horrible for someone who was used to it, but pain has a way of sapping strength out of a person. The distance may as well have been three times what it was if a man traveled it pulling a cut foot with a lame one.

"Yes, my king, I'm afraid they are. When I got here, Joseph was leaving to look for his brother. Simeon had left while Joseph slept, I assume to save his little brother from whatever he planned to do next."

Tibian's knees trembled as this extra weight fell on his shoulders. He nodded absently and trudged his way into the stone house.

I followed him in and watched as he fell into a chair and stared at the small fire Asher had coaxed to life in the fireplace. I'm sure his feet were fiery balls of pain at the ends of his legs, but for the moment, he was too tired to tend to them.

Chapter 15

Only a fool would underestimate a man with nothing to lose.

-Musings of the Historian

Asher didn't seem fazed at all by the news or by the walk. He busied himself around the house, gathering a pot here, some water there.

Soon, he had scratched together a fair soup out of the materials we had on hand and ladled it into three mugs, one for each of us.

I sipped at mine, savoring the beefy flavor of the broth. He had added the dried beef even before the water had boiled, giving lots of time for the flavor to seep throughout the soup.

Asher slammed his down as if he were due to leave again any moment. Nothing ever slowed the man down, even a little. Asher was a driven man.

The mystery I couldn't quite unravel was what was driving him. He wanted something out of all this. But what could a man like Asher want?

I doubted money held any appeal for him. A man with his morals and his abilities could have all the money he could lay his hands on, literally.

The story he had told the brothers about owing their father a debt had been compelling, but it was falling apart now that he had followed the king instead of the brothers.

I turned it over in my mind without success as Asher rose and walked over to the king. Tibian sat, staring into the fire, holding his untouched soup in both hands.

Asher reached out and smacked the king up the side of his head. Tibian thrashed like a man dowsed with cold water, sloshing his soup in the mug.

Miraculously, none spilled. Tibian looked up at Asher in shock and anger. Asher pointed at the soup.

"Eat, your majesty." He commanded as if Tibian were a raw recruit. "Your body needs to heal itself and it can't do that on an empty stomach. Eat."

Tibian sucked meekly at the broth, too broken in body and mind to object to following orders. As the warm liquid worked its way through him he seemed to awaken to how hungry he was. The rest of the soup disappeared rapidly, chunks of meat and vegetable rushing by his teeth with barely a chew to send them on their way.

As soon as the soup was gone, his exhaustion hit him as solidly as the hunger. No sooner had he set the mug on the table than his head began to droop and his eyelids began to sag.

Asher hit him again.

"See to your feet, boy!" He snapped. "Bloody things will rot in the night if you don't get your cuts cleaned out."

A belly full of warm soup gave Tibian enough spark to glare balefully at Asher. Still he obeyed and Asher bent to help him unwrap his bloody makeshift bandage. The wound was shallow, but ugly.

I guessed a sharp branch had stabbed clear through his

shoe and into his foot. The raw gash was more rip than cut.

The king gritted his teeth against the pain as he and Asher poured water over the wound and picked out slivers and bits of dirt and gravel that had worked their way into the open skin.

When it was cleaned to his satisfaction, Asher applied a foul smelling salve from a tiny jar and wrapped it in a clean bandage, ripped from a clean sheet belonging to Joseph and Simeon.

He rubbed some of the same salve on the swollen ankle as well. A quick rip of a sheet and soon the ankle was bandaged too, a light compression pushing back against the swelling.

He instructed the king to sleep with the ankle slightly higher than the rest of his body so the swelling would go down faster.

It took a moment for Tibian to arrange himself, trying to get the various limbs into the right positions without causing himself any more pain. As soon as everything was in its place, he was snoring.

I expected Asher to settle down as well, but he sat by the king, staring me down. It took me a while to understand. He wasn't about to go to sleep first. In the excitement of the day, I forgot that I should also be fairly tired.

I made a show of yawning and offered Asher the other bed. He shook his head and continued to stare me down. Pretending apathy, I laid down and went through all the motions of someone tossing around, trying to get comfortable.

Finally settling on one position, I let my breathing go deep and steady. After an hour or so of waiting like this, I heard Asher get up and move outside.

I laughed silently to myself. Even having assured himself I was sleeping, he still wasn't going to risk falling asleep in my presence. Of course, this made the mystery surrounding Asher that much deeper.

The only other thought that had made any sense was that Asher was actually a patriot, and loyal to the king. And yet, when he didn't trust me enough to fall asleep in my presence, he was still comfortable leaving me alone with his sleeping king. Nothing about Asher added up.

Still, there was no way of knowing how long he might be watching or when, so I settled in with my thoughts to wait out the night.

When morning came, Asher let the king sleep long after the sun had risen. He worked around the house, gathering what supplies had been left behind and packing them all carefully. Our departure from the camp by the clearing had been hasty. Asher took the time now to pack for a long campaign.

When the king awoke, Asher had a simple breakfast ready for him, though if you get the image of a helpful butler in your mind, you couldn't be much further off the mark.

The food was shoved at Tibian and Asher sat nearby, crouched and staring, willing the king to eat faster.

In the end, the king couldn't eat fast enough and Asher opened up business while he was still washing down the last of the bread.

"So what are you going to do next? How will you take back the kingdom?"

Whatever spark Tibian had started to show after a good night's rest faded away and he hung his head sullenly. Though he had just woken up, he looked as tired as he had the previous evening.

"I don't know. I guess it's pretty hopeless. Maybe we need to accept that."

Asher hit him, an open palmed strike to the side of Tibian's face, and if you picture a slap, you're likely the sort of person who pictured Asher as a butler.

"Now what the devil are you..."

Asher hit him again.

"Enough!" The king roared and jumped to his feet. Or at least he tried to jump to his feet. With both legs lame, it was more of an upward stumble, but he bore the pain bravely.

He set himself in his stance, hands up and ready to block the next blow. Rage and indignation contorted his features. Asher smiled a rare smile.

"Now that is what we need. If you can feel anger at a little swat like that, where then is your anger at the men who stole your kingdom and butchered your friends?"

This brought Tibian up short. Even as his face reddened after Asher's blows, his jaw began to set and his lips set in a firm line. He nodded and sat back down on the bed.

"Right you are! I'm not about to fade into the night with a whimper. I will see that an attempt is made, hopeless or not. So what do you suggest?"

"You're steering wrong again, my king. I wasn't a strategist yesterday and I'm not one now. You need to size up the situation, figure out your strengths and weaknesses and plan something that fits."

"That is the worst part of this." Tibian ran his hand

through his tousled hair. "I have no idea what's going on out there. I don't know who might have survived. Who knows? Things might not be as bad as they seem."

"Don't start to lead yourself down a fool's road." Asher had a gift for direct speech. "You must prepare yourself for the worst.

"If it's not that way, we'll all have a little laugh and celebrate, but for now you have to think that the Marauders have taken everything and are destroying the rest as we speak.

"Preparation first, hope later."

"I'll try to keep that in mind, Asher." Sarcasm crept into the king's voice, a sure sign he was feeling better. "But my real point is a valid one. We need information and we need allies. Unless you're expecting anyone to show up here, I think we need to get into the city and get some answers."

"You do know if you're recognized, you'll be killed." It wasn't a question, and it wasn't a suggestion not to go through with the plan. It sounded more like someone commenting that it might rain later.

"And who would recognize me?" Tibian's sarcastic point was well made indeed. Already he looked nothing like the king Asher had pulled from the castle.

If I had seen him in the street with his dirty peasant's clothes and unkempt beard, I wouldn't have given him another thought. His clothes smelled of smoke and old potatoes.

"Shall we take off then?" Asher was already reaching for his pack. Tibian blanched a little and shook his head.

"I'm afraid I won't be going anywhere until my foot and ankle can heal a little more. I know it would be bad to be recognized as a king, but I understand it could be just as bad being thought a beggar if the Marauders are in control."

Asher nodded, his face serious. It didn't take a Historian's instinct to realize I was missing something important.

"What would the Marauders do to a beggar? Surely it would be a good disguise."

"You really aren't from this land, are you, vagabond?" Asher's eyes turned on me again. He had been ignoring me as much as possible, but the curiosity still burned.

"The Marauders are a warrior society. They value strength and cruelty and despise weakness in any form. They have a ritual suicide if they become lame or too old to hold what is theirs. It has made them strong."

"I have heard of such societies, and I know how savage they can be. Still, they can't expect the elderly and lame to kill themselves if it is not their way."

"Oh yes they can." Asher assured me. "If one of their own clan refuses to kill themselves after their weakness has become apparent, it is seen as an even greater weakness. Such fear in one who was once brave is seen as a sickness of the mind.

"They are a superstitious race, and they move quickly to stop such things from spreading. There is no faster way to die than to beg a Marauder for mercy. He will cut you down as they would a plague victim to keep from catching it themselves.

"If they see King Tibian as a beggar, they might take his head from his shoulders on principle."

"Still, there's no time to waste." Tibian pressed. "Even if I can't make it, we still need to know if we have allies. Asher, will you go?"

Asher's first look was to me. He didn't trust me to stay with the king, but a man like that wouldn't let such an important task fall to another. He looked back to the king and nodded.

He didn't like it, but he was a true man of war. He spent no time worrying about what he couldn't change. Risks would have to be taken. He made the decision in a blink of an eye and was already past it.

"Excellent. Some of my friends may have survived. Now don't look at me like that. I won't place any false hope on it, but it would be a good place to start looking."

Asher nodded, and with no more preamble or questions, shouldered his pack and disappeared out the door. Once the decision had been made, he never stuck around for details.

The king and I kept ourselves busy over the next few days. I was pleased to note that he didn't regress to laziness now that he had a solid house and a store of supplies available to him.

He still bathed himself in well water he drew up himself. He cooked and worked around the house. Most of all, he trained long hours at everything Asher had taught him about fighting. His dedication from before had grown into a full obsession.

He worked himself through stances and rolls until sweat dripped from his brow. He found Simeon's practice sword and worked tirelessly at integrating it into his stances, dancing back and forth, blocking and parrying against an invisible, though obviously determined, opponent.

Occasionally he would stumble or wince as he came down on his injured foot the wrong way, but he always pressed on.

As the days passed, his feet became more stable as his mind became more unsettled. Asher had been gone a full ten days at that point and Tibian's face was now a permanent scowl as he glared at the empty path leading from the house towards town.

Several times he asked me if I thought we should follow Asher to town. I always responded that if Asher was all right, he would return when it was safe to do so.

If Asher wasn't all right, then it wasn't likely that the two of us would survive whatever had taken him down. The king would argue, then grumble, and eventually go back to training.

Not that I wasn't a bit impatient myself, but it was different for me. When you're in it for the story, the last thing you want is for everything to happen according to plan.

It often amazes me that people try to get their whole lives to fit into a precise plan. Even if it works, what does that prove but that you made a very dull plan?

So it was a moment of great happiness when Asher was suddenly back. Though both the king and I spent most of our days keeping an eye on the path, neither of us saw Asher until he was standing between us, like he had never left.

"What kept you?!" Tibian blurted. His surprise at Asher's appearance was nothing compared to his impatience and his hunger for some kind of news.

"I had to be thorough, my king, and I had to be careful. The kingdom is in turmoil and blood runs in the street. It's not like I could wander into a bar and ask for the latest gossip."

Tibian took the rebuke in stride and kept pressing for information.

"So what have you found out?"

Asher waved us into the house before he responded, dropping into a chair in a rare display of weariness. I wondered idly how long and how far he had walked, or how long it had been since he had slept.

"The Marauders have taken the whole of the country. There are no pockets of resistance or holding lines anywhere." Asher's words were stark and hopeless. They settled on Tibian like a cold layer of frost.

"Did the Land Guard suffer heavy losses?" He ventured. Asher scoffed.

"The Land Guard barely participated. A few squads made a decent showing for themselves, but they were no match for the organized Marauders.

"Most of the Land Guard responded by burning their uniforms as quickly as possible. Even now the vast majority of your soldiers are completely occupied doing their best farmer impressions. They are the first to line up and bow low every time a Marauder passes by.

"The Marauders are executing anyone who even appears to resist them. Worse, they have let it be known that the only way to prove your own loyalty is to inform on others.

"Anyone who even thinks about forming a resistance is being reported to the Marauders in exchange for immunity or favors.

"Of course, there aren't quite enough conspirators to go around, so many of your people are being less picky. A lot of unpopular neighbors are being reported as rebels."

Tibian looked positively sick. I didn't much like this part of human nature myself. Fear led people to do horrible things. Asher pressed on.

"There is a story or two passing around of a band of rebels

who have been saving people from execution in the last week or so. They say they are swifter than the wind itself, wear masks into battle, and never bleed."

Tibian brightened, grasping at this small thread of good news.

"Then there must be some remnant of the Land Guard still willing to fight. Perhaps more will flock to them and form a real resistance! Is there any chance of contacting them?"

Asher shook his head sadly, halting the king's exuberance.

"You don't know how these kinds of stories work, my king. These stories of supernatural abilities are those spawned when people are giving excuses as to why they lost a battle they shouldn't have. After all, who could blame you for losing to a spectral enemy?"

"What are you saying, Asher?" Tibian's look was pained. "Are you saying this band can't help us?"

"My king, I am saying there is no band. The few stories I've heard lead me to believe that they are stories made up to cover up embarrassing losses."

"But losses to whom?"

"Simeon."

The look on Tibian's face was priceless. His jaw hung slack in bewilderment and his face pinched with unasked questions. He looked like a man frozen mid-sneeze.

"What on earth are you talking about? What about Simeon?" The king finally managed to blurt out.

"I mean the Marauders are suffering losses to Simeon and the informers are failing to bring him in. So both parties exaggerate his abilities to make their failure more palatable to their superiors." Asher explained slowly, as if to a child.

"But you said there was no band of resistors, but Simeon is winning battles. Do his soldiers not count as a band? I am in no mood for word play, Asher."

"Listen carefully." Asher spoke so slowly now, he might as well have been drawing diagrams on a board.

"There is no band, there is only Simeon. He is doing this alone. That is why no one can find him or turn him in. I never said there were battles, I said they had suffered losses. Slave trains have been freed, people saved from execution, supplies stolen, that sort of thing."

"Ah." Tibian said, his face growing disappointed again. "So our band of resistance is only one man, and he is doing scarcely more than pranks."

Asher's eyebrow raised.

"Perhaps I should give an example, my king, as I don't think you understand. On one moonless night, he crept through a Marauders' death camp.

"They had spent the day rounding up those they found inferior and had them digging a mass grave. They were all due to be killed in the morning, old men, cripples, and children with defects.

"He timed four different fires with such precision that they all sprang up at once, as if an entire squad had torched the camp.

"He pulled tents down around sleeping warriors and set them ablaze as well. When the guards who had been watching the prisoners rushed to the flames, he cut them down like reeds.

"When the whole camp roused, he yelled insults about

their mothers, their honor, and possible animal contributions to their lineage. Every last Marauder grabbed a sword and chased after him into the woods.

"He led them around for almost a mile before finally bursting into another Marauder camp, yelling 'They're coming!' while managing to kick out the few lanterns they had burning.

"When the two parties met, each thought the other to be the enemy and the close fighting in the dark was brutal. They suffered heavy losses before they figured out they were fighting their own.

"By the time the survivors had made their way back to camp, even the oldest, slowest prisoner was long gone. So if you would describe a feat of strategy like that as a prank, you've got a lot to learn."

Tibian looked like he wanted desperately to be mad about something, but couldn't quite figure out what he could be angry about without seeming like more of a fool.

He still hated Simeon, and hearing his praises sung, especially by someone like Asher, was bad enough. Having it come as a rebuke had poured salt on the wound.

"Well at least we know Simeon hasn't given up. Any other news?" I spoke to save Tibian some embarrassment. Selfishly, I was also anxious for us to get on with our next move, whatever it may be.

"I found Tibian's steward, he says he was away from the castle when the attack came." It seemed to me that Asher was hesitant to share this last piece of news. Still, Tibian brightened with enthusiasm.

"That is amazing! Where is he? If I know Yaltus he would

have insisted on coming to me immediately. You did tell him about me, didn't you?"

"I didn't think that was my decision to make, my king. I told him I could take him to someone who knew something about where you had gone. He waits where I left him."

"Why didn't you say so?! Let us be off! I'll grab my pack, we must leave immediately." Tibian sprang to his feet, fully healed now and anxious to be off. He dashed into the house to gather supplies and Asher and I were left alone for a moment.

"You don't trust him, do you? This Yaltus, I mean."

"You forget something, vagabond," Asher's look was scornful. "I may or may not trust Yaltus, but I certainly don't trust you."

Chapter 16

War is more than battles, and battles are more than violence.

-Musings of the Historian

That did a decent job of stopping our conversation in its tracks, and the rest of our time was spent hurriedly gathering supplies for our journey.

Now that an ally had presented himself, the impatient king flew around in a fury, desperate to be doing something to reclaim his kingdom.

We were on the road in no time, Asher leading us down paths barely visible to the eye. It seemed to me that Asher was deliberately leading us through zigzags and backtracks. He didn't want anyone finding our trail back to the brothers' cottage.

The idea made sense. We had stayed there a long time and no one had found us, even by accident. It was a good place to hide and I could understand Asher's reluctance to let an asset like that slip through his fingers.

At long last, we came to a clearing where a nervous looking man sat on a log, his back to us. He was rocking slightly and fidgeting nervously as he waited, having not heard us enter the clearing yet, due to the soft grass underfoot.

He wasn't old, but his wispy hair had thinned early, leaving small patches of thin hair to blow around his scalp like cobwebs. He turned sharply when the king stepped on a dry branch, the sharp crack unusually loud in the quiet meadow.

He sprang to his feet immediately, a large smile spreading across his face. He hurried to the king to wrap him in a nervous hug, babbling the entire way.

"Oh! Your grace, your excellency! How are you feeling? Where have you been? What has been done to you? Have you heard about the kingdom? Dreadful, absolutely dreadful!

"When I stop to think about what would have happened if I hadn't... But no matter, the point is you're here now. Have you thought about what you're going to do?"

He went on for quite a while in that manner. His questions piled one on top on another, never waiting for an answer, though Tibian did his best to nod or shake his head where he could as Yaltus fussed over him, picking at his hair and clothes like a mother hen, clucking and all.

Finally, Tibian waved a hand impatiently and Yaltus stopped abruptly, looking sheepish for his informality.

"Yaltus, I appreciate your concern, and I am happy to see you as well. Right now we have pressing matters that require our immediate attention."

"Oh, of course, your majesty!" Yaltus gushed. I had now heard a total of four people use the title, "your majesty," with Tibian.

Simeon said it sarcastically, meant to wound. Joseph said it with a friendly air, as one would salute a butcher or grocer. Asher said it with a practiced formality that betrayed none of his true feelings.

When Yaltus said it, however, it truly did give the

impression of majesty. The words oozed with ceremony and deference.

"Oh, your eminence, we must get you as far away as possible and as fast as possible! I am shocked that your retainers would let you get this close to the city as it is!"

He shot Asher and me accusing looks. "The price on your head would buy a man wealth and safety from the Marauders for his whole life.

"I am ashamed to say that there are those among your own subjects who didn't understand your absence.

"Some even have the audacity to claim that you abandoned us, my lord. I know you far too well to ever believe such nonsense. It is not for these farmers and peasants to question your motives, my liege."

Once again, Tibian had to raise a hand to silence Yaltus and have his own say.

"Yaltus, I am not leaving. I intend to fight for my kingdom... and for my people. I need you to tell me what you have seen of the situation so I can know how to prepare."

The king may as well have told the steward that he intended to fly over the kingdom flapping his arms and burning the Marauders with fire from his eyes.

He stared slack-jawed at the king, voluntarily silent for the first time since I met him. When the shocked look passed from his face, he stammered and stuttered as he tried to frame a response.

"Your ma... I... you ca... if I even... you can't!" He finally blurted, then clapped his hand to his mouth, shocked by his own impropriety. He rushed to fix the situation.

"What I mean to say, my lord, is that I must have failed you. I have not described the situation well enough for the good king to understand. The Land Guard is completely dissolved.

"The people themselves have shown almost no resistance to the invaders. The situation borders on civil war as people rush to turn each other in as traitors, sire.

"Your heart is as great as your father's, but these rabble do not deserve your sacrifice! They were ungrateful to you even before the invasion, and now they have revealed themselves to be the rats they are.

"We would do best to flee this land as fast as we can and leave this nightmare behind us!"

Yaltus pleaded with his king, his hands wringing as he painted a picture even bleaker than what Asher had reported. As he listened, the muscles in Tibian's jaw worked like pulsing snakes.

An emotional torrent was raging below the surface. I couldn't quite guess what the king was thinking as his servant described the hopelessness of the situation. Luckily for me, the king did not leave me waiting long.

"Enough!" Tibian barked and Yaltus shrank back like a dog about to be kicked. "I know you are thinking of my safety, Yaltus, and I am grateful for your concern. But I will not crawl away and watch the nation my father built be ravaged!

"I will not judge my people for what they've had to endure. Every man makes his own decisions, and I will make mine. I will be a man who stands and fights to protect his own. If that means blood and death, then I welcome it!"

For the second time since I had known him, Tibian stood

147

as a king and a true son of his father. It suited him.

"I am well aware that the odds are full against us, Yaltus. If you do not wish to be involved, I will give you my leave to go, as well as my blessing.

"But I am not without strength myself. The man you see behind me is none other than Asher, hero of the Marauder wars."

"Gholost!" Yaltus gasped as his eyes flew to Asher. He had barely noticed the two of us since the meeting had begun, his eyes entirely on the king.

"The Marauders have asked after him. The price on his head nearly rivals your own, my lord. I don't know where you found him, but you are certainly correct that he is a powerful ally.

"Your other companion, is he also someone of importance?"

Yaltus' tone was hopeful as his eyes traced over me, but Tibian shook his head.

"Merely a wandering mad man who has taken it upon himself to follow me around."

He shot me a smile over his shoulder to show that all was in good humor. Yaltus' shoulders slumped in disappointment as he realized that the listing of allies was over. Tibian pressed on.

"You have obviously survived among the Marauders. I need you to tell me everything you know about their movements.

"I intend to push back. If the people see that someone is willing to fight for them, maybe they will be willing to fight for themselves."

The king's strategy was instantly familiar: it was Simeon's. Though I'm quite sure he would never admit it, it was obvious that the king saw the vision in what Simeon was doing.

148

The people needed to see that the Marauders weren't all-powerful. They needed to see their invaders be foolish, bleed, and lose. These were powerful images to an oppressed people.

Yaltus started feeble protests a time or two, wringing his hands all the while. Finally, he drew a deep breath and let it all out in a martyr's sigh.

"My liege, if this is what you wish, I am with you, though it mean my death. I will be your eyes on the inside and feed you all the information I can for your raids."

My eyebrow raised slightly as Yaltus proclaimed his willingness to fight and die with one breath, then expertly put himself out of harm's way with the next.

Still, information was what the king had asked for, and Yaltus didn't seem like he would be much help in a fight.

He had a fair paunch that pressed against his fine clothes, which was an odd contrast to his thin neck and wrists. He gave the impression of a stout tree with thin, brittle branches.

The king and his steward settled on the log and discussed how the Marauders were handling the invasion, their treatment of the slave trains and so on.

I stretched out on the soft grass and enjoyed the sunshine. For appearances, I made it look like I was sleeping a time or two, though I was careful not to miss any of the conversation.

Asher paced slowly behind the two, not paying attention to anything in particular, but missing nothing.

Finally, Yaltus mentioned something in passing that drew the full attention of the king. When the Marauders had taken the castle, they had captured the sword of Stephan, which had hung in a place of honor in the main hall.

They now displayed it in the capitol square as a trophy. Tibian latched onto the information like a dog on a bone. His enthusiasm drew Asher in closer.

"How many men guard the sword?"

Yaltus immediately looked suspicious of the king's curiosity.

"Not many, my lord, usually only two or three. Surely you can't be considering risking your life for such a trifle!" Yaltus protested.

"None could ever call the sword of my father a trifle. It served as a symbol of hope for this people for long years before I was even born. I can't imagine anything better for a first target."

"But, my liege..." Yaltus had started to babble and Tibian silenced him with a wave.

"Save your breath, Yaltus, I know what I'm doing. I know full well that I cannot win my kingdom back with one warrior. I need my people behind me.

"For that to happen, they need to know that I am still here, that I am still fighting for them. While it might be safer to skulk around and strike at easy targets, that's not going to get the job done. I need something public, something drastic."

"As you command, my king." Yaltus acquiesced. He brightened. "I overheard a Marauder commander bragging that they were going out in force to hunt down the band that is raiding their slave trains. I expect there will be few soldiers left in town tomorrow. It may be a good time to strike."

Tibian nodded and looked to Asher, who now stood at his shoulder. Asher shrugged, which was as good as Tibian was likely to get.

150

We had a plan.

The king was anxious to get things started and the next morning, we found ourselves back in the city.

I found a small alcove by a building where I could see the entire square, but no one could see me. I could see the sword clearly from where I stood. The Marauders had put together an impressive display.

They had gathered together a pile of dirt, then stacked trophies all around it. Soldier's uniforms, helmets, and swords piled on top of one another, forming a rusting and fading pile of the nation's military relics.

At the top of the pile, the former king's sword stood brightly, standing up in the dirt at the top of pile. It formed the peak of the pyramid.

Two large and menacing men stood to either side of the pile, discouraging anyone who might be tempted by the easy loot.

Asher and the king approached from the far end of the square, walking slowly. The guards took little notice of them, or anyone else for that matter.

While these men were obviously capable warriors, they looked more than a little bored with the mundane guard duty they had been assigned.

As soon as they were within a few paces, one of the guards waved a hand dismissively and barked a casual insult. Asher flung his hand out and a knife appeared, sunk deep into the man's chest.

The burly warrior looked confused as he stared at the handle of the knife, trying to figure out how it had gotten there.

He reached up a hand to pull it out, instinctively, but

found that he had no strength. He then collapsed like a puppet with its strings cut.

His companion recovered quickly from the shock and leaped at Asher, sword in hand. The mighty downward strike he aimed at Asher would have felled a young tree.

It hit hard on the stones of the square as Asher moved down and through the strike, passing under the blade. As the bigger man's momentum carried him past, Asher clenched both fists together and slammed them hard into the man's side.

There is a particular look a man gets when he has broken ribs. The elbows tuck in tightly, as if trying to keep warm. The face gets a pained expression and freezes there as the brain forbids the body to move or even breath. The sharp pains in the core awaken something very raw in the primitive brain, a sense of being broken.

The Marauder guard displayed all of these symptoms and emotions in a flash, but had no opportunity to coddle his broken ribs. Asher lashed back with another strike, planting his foot hard and fast into the lower back of the larger man.

Broken ribs or no broken ribs, the wrenching pain in his back tore a scream out of the warrior as he fell hard to the stones of the square and held himself there as still as he could manage.

At least, I think that is what he was doing. The pain or the strike to the spinal cord may have rendered him unconscious, it was hard to tell at that distance.

The scream commanded the attention of everyone in the square. The common people drew back, afraid to be spotted at a scene of trouble.

Three stray soldiers came running across the square at

Asher. They slipped naturally into a battle formation as they ran, even though they hadn't been together when the violent fracas began. Effortless teamwork has always been the mark of trained soldiers.

As Asher moved to the attack, Tibian crawled quickly to the top of the pile and pulled his father's sword free. He threw back the hood that had obscured his face. He raised the sword to the sky and roared his defiance at the oncoming Marauders.

Of course, the king's part in the battle was purely symbolic. He would not participate in the actual fighting.

As the three closed on Asher, he sidestepped their charge and came at the one on the left.

The other two suddenly found themselves cut off from the action by their own comrades and pushed and dodged to get around each other. In this confusion, Asher spread destruction like a natural disaster.

Earlier in my tale, I spoke briefly about my experience with master fighters. I spoke of grace and elegance, of their violence approaching a dance as they wove their way through combatants. I want one thing to be perfectly clear:

Asher was nothing like that.

Although I had seen him move with fluid grace, there was nothing graceful when Asher got down to real fighting. His style was harsh and brutal. His stances were perfect, he was never off balance and never out of position.

From this platform of power he stomped and snapped and ripped his way through the three men. Rather than clean deaths, Asher dealt in the trauma of breaking bones and wrenched joints.

In a mere matter of seconds, only one of the Marauders

was even able to close his hand around his sword, and he couldn't stand on the mangled mess Asher had made of his knee.

Asher stood back and laughed. It was a dark sound, full of arrogance and disdain. I understood in a whole new light why the Marauders had named him Hunger.

He didn't just kill men, he broke them. He shattered their bodies and minds and left them with laughter in their ears.

The people around the square stared with horror and confusion on their faces. Tibian moved quickly to change their focus.

"My people, I am King Tibian!" He shouted his name as a challenge, a threat to be answered.

"These mongrels have taken what is mine while my back was turned. For that I owe each and every one of you a grave apology. But these Marauders deserve only my rage! For I am a man, and I am your king!"

He thrust the sword again into the air, then ran down off the pile and followed Asher away from the square. The Marauder guards left in Asher's wake shifted and groaned.

The gathered people milled restlessly, as if in shock. I imagine it was hard for them to process what they had seen. They feared the Marauders, but it was hard to run from five men lying on the ground, at least one of them dead.

Finally, one man slipped quietly away through an alley. The rest seized on the idea and the crowd dissolved in seconds, each going their own way as if nothing had happened.

In under a minute, the square was completely deserted except for the groaning Marauder soldiers. At that, I slipped away myself to rejoin the king.

154

When we regrouped outside of town, the king was exultant, as if they had managed to defeat the whole Marauder army, rather than a few disorganized guards. Asher was stone faced, as if he had just finished picking out a cabbage from a market stall.

"That was incredible!" The king exclaimed. "I know Yaltus said most of the soldiers would be gone, but I'm still amazed it went so smoothly.

"I swear my heart is beating like a drum. I honestly went into that prepared to die. Do either of you ever feel that way?"

"Always." Asher responded simply.

"Never." I shrugged. The reader might find this a bit flippant, but things had gotten to the point where it didn't much matter what I said. Tibian had convinced himself that I was more than a little mad, though harmless.

Asher was similarly convinced that anything I said could not be trusted. So with that kind of freedom, I enjoyed the luxury of almost always telling the truth.

Once I even commented that their stars seemed a bit pinker than some others I'd seen; both of them had rolled their eyes at me.

"Do you think he'll hear about it?" Tibian's attitude had become subdued, his question a confession he didn't quite want to make.

While he thrilled at his symbolic victory, the true aim of his design hadn't left his mind. He needed Simeon. What he expected from him, I couldn't quite say, but his former captor had become something for him to believe in.

In his mind, Simeon represented the answers to the

155

questions the king could not answer for himself.

"Sooner or later. I imagine." Asher replied. The thrill of battle was already over for him and he was back to looking bored and watchful. "We'll have to keep up the pressure, make sure he knows we haven't been killed."

"How will he contact us?"

"The only location we all have in common is the brothers' house. He will leave us some sort of sign there. We will leave a sign in return. Finally we will meet there once we're sure we won't be ambushed."

Tibian nodded, comforted that there was a plan.

Chapter 17

There is an undercurrent of savagery in the human psyche. Anyone who forgets this and doesn't guard against it, risks being swept away by it.
    –Musings of the Historian

What came next was a variety of strikes. Unlike Simeon, who used strategy and guile to trick the Marauders into thinking that he was an entire team of men, the attacks made by our little group were done in plain sight and relied almost exclusively on Asher.

The point wasn't to build a myth of an armed resistance, but rather to remind the Marauders of the horrors that Asher had visited upon them in the first war and bind that image with the king.

Above all, it was showing the people that their king still existed and had powerful allies.

The targets for these attacks were consistently small, but highly visible. Simeon usually freed slave trains or sabotaged supplies.

Asher would ghost his way up behind a Marauder captain in the middle of a square and kill him in front of everybody. It was a shock and awe campaign, meant only to destabilize, not to conquer.

The locations and schedule of these targets were fed to the

king by Yaltus, who never lost an opportunity to crow over some small success or lavish praise on the king. Even Tibian got tired of it at times and ordered the sycophant to be quiet.

Yaltus always immediately complied, shutting his mouth with a pop, only to open it seconds later to apologize to the king and thank him for his patience and long suffering.

Asher's mood grew dark any time Yaltus was around, and he openly scowled when Tibian talked with his steward about their plans.

Of course, there was little he could actually say beyond his personal dislike of the man. The fact was that the intelligence he gathered for us was always accurate and timely.

It had been enlightening for me to watch Asher in battle, the man cracked bones like a chef cracked eggs, easily and without a second thought.

After a while, I got used to his peculiar brand of brutality and figured that I had seen what I needed of Asher.

Then the day came when Yaltus told us about a certain slave caravan that had been stranded by a washed out road in the previous night's rain storm.

"How many guards?" Tibian asked, weighing the options in his head. It wouldn't be public, like the others had been. Still, the idea of his people in chains had a disturbing effect on him, having been held captive himself.

"Around ten." Yaltus replied.

"Can you handle ten, Asher?"

Only I was close enough to see a gleam in Asher's eyes. Whatever he was thinking, he didn't share it with the group.

"Maybe, but only if I go alone."

"Alone?" Tibian repeated back, a little stunned. In the public attacks, Tibian being there had always been a key element.

"Yes, I can't go into a battle like that keeping track of anyone else, I need to focus."

There was a growing suspicion in my mind that focus wasn't what Asher was after.

"I would like to come along. It would surely help our cause for the people to see me." The king protested.

"It wouldn't do much for our cause if you got skewered like a pig on a spit, boy." Asher reprimanded him. "You focus on the war, leave this battle to me."

"Fine." Tibian bit the end off of the word, turning his back on Asher in frustration. It would be hard on him to sit and wait in camp.

He thought of something and turned around to make another argument.

Asher was already gone.

Tibian turned back to the fire, knowing the moment was lost. I followed Asher's example and ducked into the trees as soon as Tibian's back was turned.

I wanted to see what Asher had planned for the ten Marauder men.

Following Asher through the woods was hopeless, the man was nothing more than a whisper in the woods and he had a head start on me. Luckily, Yaltus had told everyone the location of the stranded slave train and I rushed ahead to get there before Asher.

The setup was typical enough for soldiers who had been given an unexpected day off. While they waited for reinforcements to come help them move their wagons, the warriors lounged, wasting their time at gambling with each other for small stakes.

One soldier was placed as sentry over the slaves and he paced back and forth amongst them. Two others were stationed as lookouts, each about a hundred yards away from the others on either side of camp.

When Asher struck, he attacked one of these outer sentries. The man was leaned up against a tree, his arms folded as he tried to see what was happening with the game back at the wagon.

Asher came around the tree like a specter, pulling the man's sword from his belt.

The man turned to meet this attack and Asher struck him hard across the jaw. Stunned, the man hit his back against the tree behind him, using it to steady himself. Asher drove the man's own sword into his stomach and into the tree behind him, pinning him there.

Asher could have killed the man quietly, but stealth wasn't on the agenda today. The other men at the wagon were now scrambling for their weapons as they heard their comrade's screams for help.

A brave sort, the pinned warrior made a few attempts to strike out at Asher, reaching for his belt knife. Without breaking eye contact, Asher slapped his hand away and grabbed the knife for himself.

Running footsteps pounded behind Asher, but he did not look around to see his attackers. He kept looking into the Marauder's eyes until the lights went out behind them.

160

Satisfied, he turned to meet the charge of men. Of course, it wasn't much of a charge. When the men were close enough to see what was happening, they slowed and spread out, instinctively wary of this demon exulting over his prey.

Asher did not let them get into formation. He moved laterally, facing them while his body moved sideways. His footwork kept the Marauders from coming upon him as a group.

I had seen tactics like that before. They were common with men who knew how to fight larger groups. Position became everything.

The difference with Asher was the way he moved. He was never out of his stance, his legs just moved underneath him. The effect was spider like, which only made him more unnerving and unnatural.

He lashed out suddenly. The person in front had started to move to Asher's left, trying to anticipate his movements. His assumption left his sword arm out of position.

Asher darted in like a shot. The sword clattered out of the man's hands as he clutched at his new wounds.

The closest man tried stabbing over the top of the wounded man's shoulder, hoping for a lucky strike. Asher dodged the stabbing sword easily. He brought his left hand up to catch at the attacker's wrist and jumped backwards.

The man screamed and I barely caught a glimpse of iron where the two men's arms met. Asher had hooked the other man's wrist with the climbing hooks he kept up his sleeve.

Two men went down in a pile as Asher drug the one man over the other. Almost too fast to follow, Asher snatched the sword from where it had fallen and drove it down through the two men.

A vicious axe swished at his head, but he threw himself sideways, coming up in his stance after a tight roll. He laughed out loud as he saw the horror in his enemies' faces.

He wiped his left hand over his face, smearing blood across his horrible visage. I realized in that moment what Asher had been holding back when he was with the king.

This was Hunger. This was the destroyer of men and the haunter of dreams. It couldn't be an act anymore, no one could fake that kind of madness, being lost in the blood lust.

It was something I should have known. We had talked about it. It had been implied in a hundred ways. I had even felt the truth of it in my bones. Still nothing was the same as seeing the proof before my eyes.

Asher was a monster.

Roaring like a savage, he jumped at the group again. Swords raised to meet him and he swept them aside with his arm.

A dull metallic clank when swords met his arms told me that he had more up his sleeves than just hooks, though the hooks took center stage of his assault.

Planting his knife in the chest of the leader, Asher proceeded to grab at whatever arm or shoulder was closest to him. The hooks were out in plain sight now.

As always, there was no grace or fluidity to Asher's attack. He ripped and thrashed at the men, pulling and pushing with hooks and blades. They were always off balance and bleeding and Asher stood steady among them like a machine.

The second the group started to converge, he would toss himself to the side and roll out of the way. The other lookout had finally caught up and now joined the battle, though one fresh fighter meant little in the carnage that was unfolding.

There were three men still standing, four were dead, and three more were dying slowly in the mud.

Of those still standing, only one was still unwounded. Even from a distance I could see the horror in their eyes.

Asher still laughed and growled, snapping his teeth at them as he reveled in the abandon of combat.

When they hesitated to attack, Asher reached behind his neck and flung his arm forward, chucking a throwing knife into the guard who had run in to join the battle. As he fell to his knees in the mud, the last two broke and ran.

One had taken to the woods, the other had raced back to the wagon, perhaps after a better weapon or some kind of defensive position.

Asher pursued the one at the wagon. When the survivor reached his goal, Asher was only a few steps behind him and moving fast.

When the man stopped and turned, hearing footsteps behind him, Asher didn't even slow down.

Leaping like a panther, Asher caught the man's head in both hands midair. With the entire weight of Asher's leap behind them, the two men crashed into the wagon.

Wood splintered and one of the wheels broke under the force of impact. The whole wagon creaked and leaned unsteadily. Both Asher and the guard went down amid the mud and broken wood.

Only Asher stood back up.

He turned and surveyed his handiwork. Not every warrior was dead. There were some who might even last the entire day before succumbing to their wounds.

A noble warrior would have gone around and finished them, ending their lives in mercy. Asher was not a noble warrior, and he had no intention of lessening the pain of his enemies.

He stayed around long enough to find the keys and toss them at the feet of the chained slaves. Then he turned to head back into the woods.

It was at that moment that he saw me. Our eyes locked and he changed course, heading directly for my position.

I didn't move or speak as he bore down on me, looking like a demon right out of legend. I guessed that he meant to kill me.

After what I had witnessed, I knew that he would do it happily, if only to have one less annoyance he had to deal with.

He kept eye contact the entire way as he stalked up to me, saying nothing at all. He held no weapon, but I knew he didn't need one.

When he was within a few feet, he slowed. I knew what he was feeling. He was still looking into my eyes. He would feel that something was off. He would feel confused.

He stopped right in front of me and stared me down as long minutes passed. I knew that the confusion he was feeling was the only thing keeping him from the attack, so I didn't break eye contact.

I didn't even blink.

Finally, his look changed. It was a familiar expression. I had seen it in Simeon when we first met. He wanted something from me. Something important.

Whatever it was, he didn't say. He turned and ran back

into the forest, disappearing in seconds. I hurried to get back to the king before he became suspicious.

When Asher joined us, he was wearing clean clothes and the blood had been washed from his face.

Chapter 18

The final desire of any warrior is a good death.
   –Musings of the Historian

Every day, one of us would sneak back to the house to see if Simeon had left some sort of message for us. Each day that we found nothing piled on the king's shoulders like iron weights.

Worse still was the day we found something.

It was my turn to check the house. We had arranged everything in such a way as it would be instantly obvious if something had been moved.

Asher had even gone so far as to place a dry leaf in the hinge of the door, so that if the door were opened, the leaf would be crushed.

So I made my trek to the house knowing exactly what to look for. What I found was entirely unexpected.

The house had been burned to the ground.

Most of the stone walls still stood, but the roof and everything inside it had been reduced to ash.

Fragments of branches told the story clearly enough. The house had been filled with scrap wood and set alight. I rushed back to the group to report.

Asher accepted the news stoically

"They're probably combing the woods, searching for any

trace of Simeon's resistance band. Likely they're torching anything that looks like it might serve as a rally point. We'll need to be even more careful."

Tibian, in contrast, did not take the news well. He sunk down onto a log and ran his hands through his hair in a gesture of frustration that had become awfully familiar.

"So how are we supposed to get in touch with him now?" He still seemed reluctant to call Simeon by name. Asher had no answer.

"What do you think, vagabond?" Shockingly, the question, directed to me, came from Asher. It took me a moment to realize he was being serious.

All I could think was that in Asher's mind, a situation he didn't understand warranted the advice of a person he didn't understand.

"It seems to me that we need to be in the same place as Simeon, and at the same time."

Tibian rolled his eyes and scoffed loudly at my absurd answer. He started a sarcastic comment, but Asher waved him silent, his eyes still on me.

"Go on." He ordered softly. In that moment, I think Asher knew something of the truth I hid from them.

"The easiest way to do that would be to attack the same target he's attacking, or at least be close enough to follow him after he runs. But we can't."

"Why not?" Tibian interrupted again, trying to understand what Asher had found interesting in my obvious observations.

"Because if we could figure it out, then so could the Marauders. We must assume that Simeon is smart enough to keep them from figuring out his movements and targets.

"So unless we are setting ourselves as more intelligent than Simeon and the Marauders combined, we can't hope that we will ever figure it out."

Asher nodded ever so slightly. I was sure then, he knew something. How much he may have guessed, I didn't know, but he was sure in that moment that I was more than the eccentric wanderer I appeared to be.

"Go on." Asher urged again, a request this time. I was committed now. It was an uncomfortable moment for me, when the line between observer and participant blurred and stretched.

"We have to take Joseph. If we have Joseph, Simeon will come to us."

"How do we know that Joseph isn't with Simeon already?" All questions came from the king now. Asher had settled down to listen.

Though I was never in real danger, I couldn't help but feel unsettled by the killer's eyes that seemed to be looking inside me. I focused on my answer to Tibian.

"The same reason Simeon left him behind in the first place. Simeon's sense of honor pushes him to carry on this war, but he has no faith that it will end in anything but death for all involved.

"He has distanced himself from his brother to protect him, and he won't reveal himself unless it's to save him."

Tibian had started to nod along, the idea starting to coalesce in his mind.

"So how do we get Joseph? We have at least heard of Simeon's actions. Joseph, on the other hand, has been a complete

168

ghost from the moment he left us."

"There is one thing that will pull him out of hiding." My gaze met Asher's and held. It was time for the idea to come from one of them. I had done enough. Asher nodded, accepting the charge.

"We say we have Simeon, then Joseph will come to us."

"Well if that works, then why don't we claim to have Joseph and go directly for Simeon?"

"Because Joseph won't know where Simeon is, but I'd bet my arm that Simeon is keeping tabs on Joseph, we wouldn't be able to fool him."

The plan was simple, but devious. We were using the brothers' love and loyalty for each other to force their mutual betrayal.

There was a small part of me that suggested I should feel shame for nudging them into such a plan, but all I could feel was anticipation.

The execution was simple enough. Yaltus told us of a planned troop movement that would have most of the Marauder warriors out of the city, save for a few guards who would be spread thin to keep the peace.

A lot of care went into the planning, but in truth, most of it wasn't needed. The first step didn't take long at all.

As luck would have it, the market was full when Asher took down the guard who stood scowling near a stall. There was hardly any commotion, and the only other guard in the square wandered over curiously to see what the matter was.

Asher took his time with the second guard and when Asher finally allowed the man to fall to the ground, the spot commanded the attention of the entire square.

All looked to Asher, but it was the King who threw back his hood and stood on a crate to let his words carry over the entire marketplace.

"It has come to my attention that Simeon, son of Ander, is a traitor! We have captured him and he confessed to helping the Marauders take our land.

"Tomorrow at this same time, we will execute him for his crimes on this very spot, as an example for any who would turn on their own people!"

The speech had its desired effect and people were already chattering amongst themselves as Asher and Tibian slipped away.

Their escape route, like always, had been thoroughly planned out. There was a lot of false leads and doubling back to ensure they weren't followed.

Back at camp, the mood was dark. Unlike other attacks, which always put the king in a fighting mood, this one created a somber feeling in everyone. We had slandered the very person we hoped would help us.

If this didn't work and Tibian failed to make things right, Simeon would find himself hunted by friend and foe alike. A lot was riding on everything working just right.

The evening passed in silence. No one spoke as we prepared and ate dinner, put out the fire, and set up our beds.

Without a word, Asher slipped into the woods to begin his routine of establishing a perimeter, setting traps for the unwary, and erasing any sign we may have left in our coming and going.

As soon as the king was softly snoring, I left my bed and crept into the darkness myself. When I was a suitable distance from the camp, I started making small noises, brushing by trees and stepping on small twigs.

As expected, I didn't have to wait long before Asher's voice came from behind me.

"What are you doing out here, vagabond?" The query in the night no longer held the malice it used to.

Asher's questions had become genuinely curious concerning me, though he didn't push the issue or let the king or Yaltus see his interest.

"I came to talk to you." I turned to address him and found myself facing a tree, its rough bark inches from my nose.

Asher had spoken from a spot where, had I tried to turn and attack suddenly, he would have been guarded. This was Asher's ultimate secret to survival, he took no chances.

"You found me, what do you want?" The voice had already moved to my left, though I hadn't heard him move. He was like a wraith in the dark. The only man I knew capable of moving quieter was myself.

"I want to know why you're here." I spoke in a whisper, careful of our precarious situation. Asher snorted.

"I am a soldier of this country protecting my king, you are a wanderer who knows nothing of our land and you ask me why I am here? Seems you should answer that question first. I think it's high time you did."

"A trade then? I will tell you why I am involved, if you tell me why you stayed with Tibian, instead of following Simeon."

"Agreed." His answer came quickly, he had expected the deal. "You first."

"Very well. I travel lands to find great stories. There is

nothing else in my life."

"That's pretty thin, vagabond. Why would you risk your life for a bit of a tale? Buy any old soldier in a tavern a few ales and you'll have all the stories you can handle."

"It doesn't work that way. I have to see them unfold. I need to be a part of them. More than that, I have no choice."

Silence answered me for long moments.

"What do you mean? Are you a slave? Who is your master, and how could he control you from such a distance? Would you like him killed?"

I smiled in the darkness at the casual offer of murder. Men at times offered to kill for their family, their country, or their closest friends. Asher offered killing like most men would offer a drink of water to a tired traveler.

"I don't know my master or if one even exists. I certainly hope there is one. All I know for certain is that I must seek out these stories, just as a regular person needs to seek out water or warmth."

Asher is one of the few people I had ever shared this with, but I knew that a man like him would understand something of compulsions.

"Have you ever tried to stay in one place, build your own story?" If it had been someone else, I would have said I heard sympathy in his voice. With Asher, it must have been something else.

"Once. Only once in ten thousand years have I ever found anything I wanted to stay for, and I couldn't."

I had slipped. There is no other explanation for it. The emotion of a hard memory had distracted me to error. Worse, I didn't even realize it until I heard the horror in his voice.

"Ten thousand years?" It was a gasp in the darkness. "Do you live on as you are, or do you carry the memory of hundreds of deaths?"

My mind reeled with the impact of what I had done. If I couldn't silence him, I would need to leave and I wouldn't see the end of this story.

I had no idea how to control the damage, but it was too late to take it back. He believed me so fully. A corner of my mind noted his immediate fixation on death. There was something there I hadn't quite connected yet, perhaps it was something I could use.

"I live on as I am, though I have reason to believe that different people see me differently. But that is enough, and I must ask that you never tell anyone."

"What do you know about what comes after? After a man dies, what happens to his soul?"

His questions were intense now, his voice close and urgent.

"I don't know, Asher, I truly don't. I have seen more death and more life than I can describe, but the curtain between them is an impenetrable barrier to me."

"Oh." The single syllable shook with emotion, I couldn't say how much the question had meant to him. I moved to turn the tables, perhaps to get information I could use to insure his silence.

"A deal is a deal, Asher. Tell me, what is your purpose here, really? I mean no offense, but nothing I know about you suggests that you are doing this out of a sense of patriotism to a king you considered killing."

"I seek death." His voice was still emotional, but the feeling was dissipating like smoke in the air.

"Whose death, Asher?" I asked, though I think I knew.

"My own, vagabond."

Chapter 19

Do all men seek redemption? I have seen too much to doubt it.

-Musings of the Historian

"That is why you are involved in all this, to get yourself killed?" I had certainly heard of men, especially older warriors like Asher who sought death, but it certainly seemed like a roundabout way to do it.

I told him so and added, "Aren't there easier ways to find death, even death in battle? You could have attacked the Marauders years ago and kept on going until you found a battle you couldn't win."

Asher shook his head.

"Listen, there is a lot I don't know. I have a hard time believing that there is a life after this one. Still, I have watched the life drain from hundreds of men in my life. I have watched as something left from their eyes.

"The first time I saw it, I was sick for days, swore I'd never kill again. I was a young man, then. It was a Marauder, separated from his band. I caught him among my father's animals, stealing a chicken for his dinner.

"The second he saw me, he attacked, no hesitation. I acted on pure reflex, striking out. It was only a trick of fate that I had an ax in my hand, having just come back from cutting wood.

"I watched him die, and felt like it was my blood soaking the ground. Congratulations from my father and neighbors made it worse. They praised me as a hero, defending my home.

"After that, they included me in the village defenses. I killed again and again. It wasn't long before I stopped feeling bad about it. It was merely something I did, like chopping wood.

"Then I met Eliana."

He paused. I had been around Asher a long time. I had heard many things from his voice, primarily disdain, cruelty, or anger. When he said the name of his wife, however, I heard reverence.

"She was so simple, so pure. She was afraid of the Marauders like a child is afraid of the dark, and she loved me with wide eyes.

"Then came a day when I heard her scream. I don't even remember running, but I was suddenly there in the field where she had scrambled against a tree, crying.

"The man who stood over her wasn't a Marauder, but a drunk farmhand. I had lost enough innocence to know what he intended.

"I broke his bones, vagabond. I crushed him, body and spirit, before I spilled his blood and stood over him.

"She rained warm kisses on my cheek and neck and told the story to all who would listen about how her love had saved her. She was far too pure a soul to see what had really happened in that clearing.

"I had enjoyed it. I enjoyed it a lot. The rage and hate boiled inside me with absolutely nothing to hold it back. My savagery had the perfect covering of righteousness, but that didn't change what it was. Once it had been unleashed, I couldn't go back to how I was. I have tried.

"My truth is that I do not feel alive except when lives are at stake. It is proper that people call it blood lust, for I hungered for it like a beast after his mate.

"Eliana never stopped believing in me. Of course we were married and she stayed by my side as long as I let her.

"When I was banished from the army, it was my last chance at redemption. I could have settled down and spent my life with her."

His voice broke and we sat in silence while he gathered himself. The story had all the emotion of a confession; and confession it was.

Asher knew the demon he had become. Like an addict who sees the ruin of his own life, he felt the horror of it, but didn't have the strength to change. Finally he spoke again, his voice still full of emotion, but under control.

"I didn't, of course. I couldn't face the life of daily toil with ax and plow. Eliana still didn't doubt me. She sent me off with tears in her eyes and a smile on her face, telling me how proud she was of me.

"Her words haunt me to this day, but I would never have missed a syllable of it. She could almost make me believe it, that I was a noble warrior, devoted to the safety of all.

"By the time the war ended, I had soaked myself in blood. Coming home was like coming out of a dream, a nightmare where I was the monster.

"Eliana thanked her gods for my safe return and bragged to all who would listen that her husband, the great war hero, had come back. To hear her tell it, you would think I threw out the Marauders single-handedly.

"She could have saved me, I believe. With no war and her love, I may have salvaged some part of my soul. I'll never know for sure. I was home less than a year when she died in childbirth, the child with her.

"All my experience with death wasn't enough to prepare me for that. I was there when the light left her eyes, like I had seen so many times before.

"In that moment, death made me sick, like the first time. This time, there was no end to it. She had gone where I couldn't follow.

"If there is a life after death, I must go there. Surely there is no death there, and she must be there. But I cannot return to her a coward. To see shame in her eyes would make eternity a darkness.

"If I threw myself into a battle I couldn't win, how is that different than cutting my own throat? No, I can't see her like that. It must be something she would be proud of.

"I tried to find it in the slums, fighting battles for the wretches. But there was nobody there who could kill me. I needed a cause, a righteous war.

"I followed the brothers because I figured they would start the kind of trouble that brought about great battles. I didn't expect the Marauders' invasion, but that only made it better in my mind.

"Simeon is fighting his battles, but he's too careful, and too good to leave me in a position for my final stand.

"This king, Tibian, has a good heart and will make a good king, if he lives. But he is also fool enough to get himself into some

178

very big trouble. All I have to do is keep him in the fight and wait for my moment."

"What makes you think he's a fool?" I asked. Asher snorted at the question.

"Look at who he has chosen to trust. An assassin, a nameless vagabond, and a simpering rag of a steward. It is something of a miracle we haven't been slaughtered already."

I chuckled, though it hadn't been intended as a joke.

"You have a point. The long odds make it a fascinating story. I guess in some way, we're here for the same reason."

"I suppose so," he mused. "Not that it matters much. Now get back to camp, the morning will come soon enough."

"Agreed."

With my new understanding of Asher and his role in all of this fresh in my mind, I returned to camp to mull it over for the rest of the night.

The new day brought old worries and no one said much of anything until the evening drew close. Asher spent a disturbing amount of time sharpening various knives that he tucked back into various folds of his clothing.

It made his stealth all the more impressive that he could do it loaded down like that. While he never showed them, I now knew about the hooks he carried up his sleeves. In many ways, he had more in common with machine than man.

Yaltus even made a small appearance, pleading with the king to hold back, to not put himself in danger. When it was obvious his concerns were being ignored, he excused himself and huffed his way back toward the city. We followed soon after.

The king and I hid ourselves in an empty hut on the

outskirts of town.

It was a storage hut for firewood, but the long winter had left it empty. Asher left us there as he took a look around. He returned quickly and nodded to the king.

"Looks like the price on your head still has plenty of takers. There is only one sleepy guard in the market, but entire squads are hidden in the alleys all around the square. If we were to show ourselves for a moment, we'd be cut down from all angles."

Tibian nodded.

"It's about what we expected. I certainly hope there are at least fewer wagging tongues than there used to be. Still, we shouldn't put much trust in that dream just yet. So how are we going to find Joseph in all this?"

"Simple enough. He's not going to let himself be seen either, but he'll want to be close enough to try something stupid when we go to execute his brother.

"That leaves a small number of places he can hide. There, behind that stand of fruit, that corner would give enough cover while keeping him close to the action. Or, inside that house, there, with the kid selling wood to the left.

"Finally, if he got here early enough and held still for a long time, he could be hiding underneath the pile of garbage that spilled over from that refuse cart."

I looked to the cart, it having overflowed with garbage from days at the market. It reminded me a lot of the cart that Asher had used to smuggle the king out of the castle.

I kind of hoped that was where Joseph was, it would give the story a kind of balance.

180

The three of us split up to work our way around to the various hiding places. It was tricky work with all the hidden Marauder guards; not to mention the informers sprinkled liberally throughout the crowd. The only safe bet was to hide from everybody.

I worked my way closer and closer to the trash cart, keeping a hood up around my face. There wasn't really anyone in the crowd who would recognize me, which is why I was sent for the trash cart, right out in the open.

Still, Joseph would recognize me and that would ruin everything, so I kept my face always pointed away, working my way closer in jagged diagonal lines, like a man wandering back and forth between stalls.

When I finally got close enough to the cart, I let a villager bump into me and I tripped over my feet, stumbling backward before losing my feet entirely, falling into the pile of trash. I turned in the air as I fell, ready to grab hold of Joseph if he were in the rubbish.

My theatrics were wasted, however, as my hands hit only more garbage as they threaded quickly through the pile. No Joseph.

I didn't have to fake my frustration as I struggled back to my feet, muttered angrily at the man I had bumped into, then stalked off, brushing violently at my soiled clothes.

I circled back around to the abandoned house and found Tibian there. His eyes raised hopefully as I came in, but fell immediately when he saw I was alone. But we didn't have to wait long before Asher came in with Joseph's limp form slung over his shoulder.

He twitched his eyes to the door and we followed him out the back and into the woods. I paused for a moment to wonder how long the Marauders would wait in their alleys before they realized they'd been played.

Chapter 20

Nothing cripples a man so thoroughly as doubt.
–Musings of the Historian

Back at the camp, Joseph woke up with his hands tied. His eyes went wide with panic. He thrashed a moment or two until his eyes locked with the king's. Anger flashed.

"How dare you call Simeon a traitor?! You are more of a traitor than he is!"

Joseph kicked out with a foot and got lucky, catching Tibian where he crouched a few feet away. His foot caught Tibian squarely on the thigh and sent him sprawling. Only luck saved his hand from going right into the fire.

He rolled as Asher had taught him and came up in a stance, but Joseph just grinned, taunting the king.

"I know he isn't a traitor." The statement put Joseph off balance, confusion replacing anger. "It was all a ruse to flush you out. We've been trying to find you. We figured you wouldn't stay away if you thought we had your brother."

"You thought right, but I don't know what you want with me. I can't be much help and I don't know where Simeon is."

"I believe you, but I also believe that he knows where you are. We announced him a traitor and kidnapped you. We can only assume that he is going to come after us to rescue you."

Joseph twisted his face and stared up at the king. When he spoke, his tone was incredulous.

"Are you sure you've thought this through all the way? The only way you'd want Simeon is if you think he can make a difference in this war.

"If you think that, you must think he's a very dangerous man. And if you think that, you must be fairly stupid to put yourself on the wrong side of his sword."

"You may be right about that, Joseph. Though with Asher on my side, it's your brother's mind I'm more worried about than his sword.

"There's a good chance he could outmaneuver us, steal you away, and possibly leave us hurt in a big way in the aftermath. So this whole plan hinges on one thing, Joseph."

"And what is that?" Tibian leaned in and Joseph leaned back, suspicious.

"You, Joseph. We need you to help us bring your brother back in. We need to work together in this. We hear about what your brother is doing, so he still wants to fight for this kingdom. But he left you behind, which tells me he has lost hope. What do you think?"

The words hit Joseph hard. Being left behind by his brother had sent him a tragic message. He nodded and his voice quavered as he replied.

"Simeon isn't easy to understand. He was always a little different. He grew up listening to our father's stories about the war and King Stephan. We both did.

When I grew up a bit, I realized that life was more complicated than just good guys and bad guys. I adjusted to all the little gray areas of life. Somehow, Simeon never did.

"He was always smart, even smarter than you know. It

184

made him different. He saw things differently, patterns and big ideas. He spent a lot of time off by himself, walking and thinking.

"You ever know one of those people who are never really happy? Simeon was one of those. Somehow he could feel alone in a crowd of people.

"I asked my father about him a couple times. He said that some men were like that, solemn and sad deep down.

"Men like Simeon or Asher, they don't quite fit into the world they were born into. Father said that he would have to figure out his own way in the world.

"Simeon never really grew out of Father's stories. The gray areas that come with growing up didn't show up for him. He still sees the world in those terms, loyalty, bravery, goodness, and all that.

"For him, they aren't ideals you need to try to live up to, they're like laws. I don't think he could steal to save his life. It's not a choice, he can't think any other way. I think it is how he keeps himself centered in the world.

"It's why he kidnapped you. He couldn't stand by and watch the kingdom our father fought for fall to pieces, but he couldn't hurt you, either.

"Now he fights because it's what he thinks is the right thing to do. And he left me behind because he thought it was the right thing to do. And he'll kill all of you if he thinks it's what he has to do. You'd be fools to doubt it."

His narrative ended, Joseph looked off into the trees, as if he expected to see his brother show up any moment.

In that moment, I understood Joseph. I had admired his zealous loyalty to his brother, but I had always seen it like a puppy

185

following after his master. Not that there was anything degrading about that. When loyalty is based on love, neither party is subservient. Now I saw it in a new light.

Joseph was not the puppy following blindly. In his mind, Simeon was the damaged one, locked into a moral code that put shackles on his hands and blinders on his eyes.

Joseph's despair at being left behind wasn't because he needed Simeon. It was because he knew that Simeon needed him.

The whole picture took new focus; the two brothers living alone; neither one married; both of them serving in the military.

Simeon barreled through life like a man in a tunnel, only one light in the distance. Joseph kept right beside his brother to protect him from himself.

Tibian placed his hand on Joseph's shoulder.

"We need you to help us bring him back in. He needs to believe this war can be won. We can do this if we work together, but we need Simeon."

The king used the name easily. All the malice he felt toward Simeon had melted away. A common enemy and deeper understanding has a way of bringing perspective.

Joseph nodded, meeting the king's eyes again.

"What do you need me to do?"

Those seven words were music to my ears. Our team was coming back together, the wounds were healing. It was enough to make a man hope.

Tibian turned Joseph over to Asher for instruction and walked away from the fire. He settled down on a fallen tree.

He leaned down and scooped up a piece of wood that had broken off of the stump. Pulling out his knife, he started whittling.

I cannot even count the number of times that I wished that I could read minds. It would add so much more to my stories if I could know what churned beneath the surface.

For now, it was enough to know that a man carving wood right before a pivotal moment probably had a lot on his mind.

I walked over and sat down next to him, taking a moment to study his face. His brows were bunched together, as if he were concentrating on the work in his hands, though it was still far too rough to need any such focus.

"Thinking about tonight?" I tested.

He shook his head, but offered nothing more. I tried again.

"It was interesting to hear Joseph talk about his brother like that. Simeon is a complicated man."

Tibian nodded, his face scrunching a little more. I was getting warmer, but if I didn't get him talking soon, he would ask me to leave him alone. I probably only had one more try.

I looked at his face again, but there were no hints there. Then my eyes dropped to his hands as the knife worked at the wood, scraping off bark to reveal the clean white wood beneath. Then I had it.

"I wish I could have met their father. He sounds like quite a man. Probably a lot like your father, wouldn't you say?"

The hands stopped carving. I had him. He still took a few moments before speaking.

"He never wanted me to be king," Tibian confessed all at once.

"What? Surely he never said such a thing!"

"Of course not, but it's obvious, isn't it? I had three brothers who were older than me. There wasn't a single person in the whole kingdom who ever thought that I would be king."

"No one could have predicted the plague, sire. You can't think that it reflects on you personally."

"I know that you're right, but it doesn't feel that way. I was old enough to see how my father treated the crown prince. He was so proud of him.

"He included him in everything. They went on hunts together. They discussed laws and judgments around the table after the rest of us were sent to bed.

"My brother was ready to be king, he was trained to be king. I wasn't trained to be anything. I was nothing more than an afterthought."

Everything started to make more sense to me. How a person sees themselves determines so much of their actions.

Tibian had idolized his father and his brother, the crown prince. He had seen them as something special, higher than himself.

When he was forced to step into their shoes, he didn't believe that he could. So he did what men often do when they feel unworthy.

He hid.

He stayed inside his walls and surrounded himself with a buffer of friends. By avoiding any interaction with the people, he kept them from finding out his secret, that he didn't belong on the throne.

"And Simeon..." I prompted.

"Simeon knew it. From the first time he looked me in the eyes. He knew I was nobody, practically an imposter on the throne."

"He didn't see you that way." I objected.

"It hardly matters if he did or not, Storyteller. The fact remains. This kingdom would be a lot better off if someone like Simeon were its king."

The rest of the pieces fell into place. Tibian's hatred of Simeon had been more than feelings of anger at the kidnapping or harsh treatment. In the king's mind, Simeon represented his own deepest failings.

Tibian carried fears and insecurities about his own abilities. By his own example, Simeon had held up a mirror to the king and proved every fear to be true.

"You're wrong, my king," I reassured him. "Simeon isn't the man to lead this country. Men like him are like stone walls, absolute and immovable.

"A good king must have that strength as well, but he must also be able to adapt, to become what his kingdom needs him to be. I have seen you change already, and there is more potential in you yet.

"You may not have been groomed for the throne, Tibian, but you are still Stephan's son. Simeon himself said so."

"Really? I suppose that's at least something. I guess I can scc your point about a king needing to be adaptable. But even if Simeon shouldn't be king, I still think someone else might be a better choice."

"Now is hardly the time for such thoughts, your majesty. The fact is that you are king. What kind of king you are is still up to you."

"I guess we'll see, won't we?"

Chapter 21

I do respect clever.

-Musings of the Historian

My only job that night was to keep out of sight. The body count had to be just right. Nothing could have pleased me more, as it gave me the chance to sit back and watch the whole scene unfold. I had to say I was proud of Tibian, it was the perfect trap for a master strategist.

The captive was tied up by the fire, a hood over his head. No guard was posted, but anyone who knew anything about that camp had to know that Asher wasn't far away. It was a lovely trap, the bait in plain view, but no way to know where the ambush would come from, if it came from the camp at all.

There was no way for Simeon to know where Asher was, and no way to defeat him in direct combat. It simply made too many variables to be accounted for. Simeon would have to change the rules of the game to win.

The attack came during the deepest hours of night, long after the lights had gone out in the tent and the fire had burned down to dim flickering embers.

True to form, Simeon's attack was nothing I expected. There was no stealth or intrigue.

There were three angry Marauders crashing through the

woods heading right for the camp.

How exactly he orchestrated it, I didn't know, but it did an amazing job of throwing the camp into confusion. A tousled figure staggered from the tent, King Stephan's sword in hand to meet the onslaught as the raging Marauders broke the tree line and stormed into camp. I tore my eyes from the scene to watch the back of the tent, where I suspected Simeon would be.

Sure enough, I could make out the barest outline of a figure crouched at the back of the tent, his hands moving like a man cutting something.

In seconds, Simeon was dragging another bound figure from the back of the tent and threw him over his shoulder before running back into the darkness. I followed, leaving the sounds of combat at the fire behind me.

Simeon did his best to stay quiet as he rushed through the trees, though it is a hard thing to do while carrying another man and by moonlight. After a while, he stopped running and walked for another couple miles in the dark.

The burden on his back made no sound, except for a mild grunt when jostled, as if he were gagged. He only stopped when he came to his own fire, set in a natural dip in the landscape, surrounded by thick brush. It was so well hidden, a man might have tripped over it before he saw it.

I nestled myself in amongst the brush where I was well hidden, but could still see and hear everything.

Simeon set his load down propped up against a log and pulled the hood off. He staggered back as the face he revealed was not his brother, but Tibian.

He stammered as he tried to wrap his mind around what

had happened.

"S–so my brother... So he was the one by the fire? But why would you be tied up? Oh no, did I unleash Marauders on my brother while his hands were tied?!" Simeon was horrified.

"Don't worry." The king hurried to console him. "That wasn't your brother by the fire. That was Asher."

"Asher?" Simeon was incredulous.

"Yes, and I suspect those Marauders were even more surprised than you were when he came off the ground, free of his bonds. My guess is that all three were disposed of before your brother even got a cut in."

"So Joseph was the one coming out of the tent? He was pretending to be you?"

"That's right. How did you know we switched?"

"The hood. You barely needed to keep him tied up. With Asher in the forest, there was no real chance of escape anyway. The only point of a hood would be to hide his identity from me.

"You still needed to keep an eye on him, which left the tent. That left Asher in the woods to spring the trap, the storyteller as the bait, and you guarding Joseph."

"Sounds like you had it about right, we just all switched roles."

Simeon nodded ruefully, a strategist beat at his own game.

"I knew I could handle you at the tent, so all I needed was something to draw Asher's attention so I could make my getaway. The only thing I could think of to break Asher's focus was Marauders, so I got some."

"It was an amazing attack, Simeon. You even pulled one over on Asher. Your only failure was your own success. We knew you'd outsmart us, so we set up our failure to be what we wanted it to be.

"The question is now what? My bonds are real enough. I am at your mercy. You can go 'rescue' your brother now, you can fade back into the woods to carry on your suicide mission, or you can take a moment and listen to me."

Simeon paused, considering. The setup had been perfect. It showed him that his brother was fine, but more than that, it showed the king's resolve and ingenuity.

Simeon needed a reason to believe that there was hope. That night's gambit must have been enough, because he nodded and settled back on a log to listen to the king. Tibian jumped right in.

"Here's how I see things right now. I have a war on my hands. It is an offensive war, but fought on my own soil. I can pick and choose my targets and I have a perfect striking force in Asher. What I don't have is a general.

"I need someone who can see the big picture and give me a plan for getting our country back, or at least weaken the Marauders enough so that our own people have a chance of getting into the fight. Will you be my general, Simeon?"

Simeon didn't respond, lost in thought.

"Come on, I'll carve you something really pretty." Tibian winked. Finally the absurdity of the situation hit Simeon and he laughed out loud.

Here was a king, bound hand and foot, bribing his general with trinkets to join in a doomed war. I couldn't help but smile myself.

"All right, let's get you back to camp. I can't say there's

really much I can offer, but since everyone seems to be dead set on getting themselves killed, we might as well finish this together."

Simeon cut the king loose and the two of them made their way back to camp where Asher and Joseph were waiting. I was waiting there too, but only because I had sped on ahead to be there when they showed up.

Joseph hugged his brother and even Asher seemed pleased, or at least as pleased as Asher ever was.

The Marauders had already been taken care of, and everyone agreed that it was already far too late to do anything else constructive. Everyone found a place to settle down and slept until morning.

The morning council was a somber affair. The king insisted we wait for Yaltus, who was late. He stumbled into the camp site looking even more ruffled than usual from his jaunt through the woods.

He mumbled elaborate excuses while he searched for a place on the log by the campfire that was clean enough. Not finding one, he let out a quiet martyr's sigh and sat down to the right of the king.

"We need a plan." Tibian started the meeting directly. "Yaltus, Simeon, you two haven't met yet, but it is important that the two of you work together.

"Simeon is my general." The king explained to Yaltus. The spindly man cast a despairing eye on Simeon. He had been living as a guerrilla fighter, and sticks and mud still clung to his clothes and scraggly beard where he had daubed it on as natural camouflage during his raids.

"Yaltus is my steward. He has been supplying us vital information about the enemy. We owe our lives to his discretion."

The steward preened like a cat under the praise of his king and started blubbering his thanks and adoration. Tibian silenced him quickly, aware of how quickly Yaltus' tongue could flap out of control.

"Somehow we must combine these two strengths into a war strategy that will allow us to regain control of the kingdom. Or..." he added ruefully, "at least get into a position where we can actually put up a fight.

"Asher, let's start with you. I know we all have some experience with the Marauders now, but you have more than all of us combined. I would appreciate it if you would give us your perspective on our enemy."

Asher had been busy watching the trees and the question caught him off guard. He shrugged and stood to address the group.

"Marauders are a tribal people. All of them feel incredible loyalty to their own local tribe. The strength of the tribe is valued above everything else. This loyalty makes the Marauders very hard to fight as a people.

"You could defeat fifty tribes, and the very next tribe would still consider itself undefeated. They don't hesitate to fight to the last man."

With that small report, Asher sat back down.

"But that's not what we're seeing now. We weren't invaded by one tribe. This is an entire army. How did they get so many tribes to work together?"

"It's a fair question." Asher nodded, thinking it over. "As I said, strength is everything. Just as they see cowardice like something that can be caught like a sickness, they also want to congregate around the strong.

"It happened often enough during the war. One headman would win a great victory and other tribes would join with him on his next raid to share in his strength.

"Still, I have never seen anything on this scale. If there is one headman at the top of this army, he must be something truly magnificent."

Out of the corner of my eye, I saw Yaltus give the tiniest nod of his head. It was so faint, it must have been a subconscious reflex. Tibian saw it too.

"Yaltus." The other man jerked like a wooden puppet and stared blankly back at the king. Tibian prompted him. "Can you tell us anything about their leader?"

"No, sire... That is to say yes, sire. At least, I can tell you what I've heard. It's only bits and pieces, you understand. Half is just babble, half is drunken bragging, and half is scared people trying to scare each other more. I scarcely feel it is worthy of my great king's time to listen to such gossip, my liege."

"Tell me anyway, steward." The king's voice held an edge that quelled any more protests from Yaltus.

"As you wish, my lord. They say he has never been defeated. They say he regularly holds entire tournaments where he is the only competitor against all comers. Some say he is better than Gholost himself."

The awkward man shot a furtive glance over to Asher, worried he might have been offended at this slight against his own legend. Asher, as usual, looked bored. Yaltus plowed on.

"He won his first fight against a full warrior when he was fourteen. He was headman of his own tribe by twenty, and he has been running small wars and raids among the Marauders ever since. With every victory, more tribes joined him, even those he had beaten. That's where this army came from."

"Does he have a name?" The question came from Asher. Yaltus cringed slightly, as he did every time Asher addressed him directly.

"I can only assume he does, noble Asher, but I haven't heard anyone call him anything but Master."

"Master?" Simeon's voice finally chimed into the discussion.

"Yes, as near as I can tell, the way they use it, it's like a king, but more. It seems to denote a physical power as well as political authority."

"So we cut the head off." Joseph suggested. "If we kill him, won't the rest of them go back?"

"It's not enough." Simeon spoke up, taking his turn to add to the discussion. "I have been fighting the Marauders on my own for weeks now.

"I had noticed that each band was a little different. Each wears their armor in a different way, uses different curses, and other little things like that.

"One of the reasons I was able to be so successful in my raids is that these different bands didn't really work together. They didn't even know each other half of the time.

"Now that Asher has explained their culture, I understand that I was seeing different tribes. Whoever this Master is, he hasn't taken the time to integrate his army. Each tribe only interacts with its own people.

"I have used this to great advantage, playing them off one another in my raids. Even if they don't actually fight each other, the confusion while they sort things out usually gave me ample time to make my escape.

"The problem with killing the Master would be that none of these tribes would see it as a personal loss. All that would happen is that they would feel freer than ever to loot and kill. Right now, fear of the Master is the only thing keeping them leashed.

"If we kill him, we won't have one army to deal with, we'll have dozens of tribes all going berserk in our lands. It would be pure devastation."

"What do you suggest, Simeon?" Tibian asked.

"It seems like this whole thing is held together by the impression of this man's strength. More than killing him, we need to make him appear weak. If we can create doubt in the minds of the Marauders, it may spark internal rebellions.

"The Master would need to crack down on his own people to secure his position. If we can pull it off, this army will start to implode on itself.

"Enough disorder will break the yoke of fear that holds our own people back. We might be able to organize enough fighters to make attacks on whoever is strongest. As they are being taken down by other tribes, we can shift our focus to whoever is next. We can fight our battles without ever being the primary target.

"It would be a delicate balance. We would actually defeat ourselves if we had a big, decisive victory. It would either unite them against us, or shatter them into roving bands, burning and murdering through our country. We must walk a thin line."

Heads were nodding around the fire. It was a crazy, desperate kind of plan, far too dependent on luck. It was exactly the kind of plan a band such as this needed. A chance in the dark.

"So how do we make the Master appear weak? It sounds like any fight with him is going to be life or death." Joseph spoke the obvious. It was Asher that answered.

"Poison. It's hard to respect a man's fighting ability while his body withers and he retches and screams. The right dosage would keep him alive and able, but not as he was."

The king and Joseph both looked uncomfortable at the nature of the plan. Something in their personal honor balked at the treacherous nature of poisoning a man.

Simeon and Asher had no such qualms. The absolute morals in the one and the absolute lack of morals in the other had prepared them to do whatever was necessary.

In the end, there was no real way around it. Their chances were fairly slim as things stood. Nothing else made much sense. Any discussion about the morality of the thing was supplanted by the conversation about how to do it.

"So how do we get poison into his food? Or is there another way of getting it into him?"

"The food would be the best way of controlling the dose. Wine would be even better, as the stuff the Marauders drink already tastes a bit like poison." Asher commented.

"There are poison darts and things like that, but there is a lot more risk of killing him accidentally. Such things would also force us to be awfully close for the act. Even if we got that close, once we stuck him, getting away from all those guards would be a tricky matter."

"So we have to get in close enough to poison his wine?" Joseph chimed in, "Seems like that will already be a fair trick."

"I can help with that." Yaltus' reedy voice came as a surprise, as everybody had almost forgotten he was there. All eyes were on him and he took a moment to smile at the attention.

"The Master has moved a lot of the stores to a different wing of the castle. It isn't guarded very well and I know their guard routines well enough to keep us out of sight. The trick is getting inside the walls.

"There is a weekly event where those who are starving gather in the castle to try and sell information for some food or gold. We could blend in with them. It is possible, however, that some of us might be recognized.

"While it pains me to put any of you in danger, I must suggest that all of us go. If one or even two get captured, the rest must finish the mission. Then, we would have everybody inside already to make diversions and attempt a rescue."

Even Simeon nodded. The importance of the mission was ultimate. Failing now would close all the opportunities now open to them.

I caught a wisp of a smile on Asher's face, or at least less of a frown. That confused me a little, but I supposed the prospect of escalating the war appealed to him.

"When is this gathering of informants?" The king asked. At this, Yaltus cringed apologetically.

"I fear, my king, the next one is tomorrow evening. After that we must wait another week, or two or three, if they cancel them as they have in the past."

"Asher, could we have the poison ready by tomorrow?"

The assassin's quiet nod suggested to me that the poison was ready now, likely tucked into one of his many pockets.

"Aren't we rushing it a little?" Joseph asked. "I don't see the harm in putting it off for a week or two to gather more information. That would give us more time to scout out the castle, maybe we could find a way for Asher to make it in alone."

"No," Simeon rebuked his little brother gently. "I know it's tempting to put this all on Asher, as his skill in getting into places is impressive. Yaltus is right, however, this is too important to risk having something go wrong. We don't know how much has been changed inside the castle.

"As for taking our time, we are already at risk. Every day we spend in the woods is one more day we might get caught and slaughtered.

"They have stepped up their patrols and search parties. Those Marauders I let into camp as a distraction were only half a mile from here. Our risk only grows greater. If I could do it tonight, I would."

Joseph nodded, bowing to his brother's superior strategic sense. There was a long pause, as if waiting for someone else to air an objection. There were none. The path was set.

There were almost no preparations to be made. As I suspected, Asher already had the poison at hand. He doled out the appropriate dose into several small bottles and gave one to every member of the party. Even I got one, though he already knew that I wouldn't play a key role in the story.

Tibian worked at making a disguise for himself, rubbing

dirt on his face and putting more rips in his clothing. He even had the foresight to gather a couple of small round stones that he put in his cheeks.

They bulged his face, making his almond face more round, and put a bit more focus on the bottom. It gave his face a drooping quality, like a hound dog.

Even Asher approved of his efforts. If a person didn't already know it was him, it would have been hard to connect the image of this dirty, sorrowful peasant to the king.

At last, however, there was nothing to do but wait. Yaltus had scurried off again, as he did to maintain appearances, lest he be gone too long and someone start to suspect. They all agreed to meet at the castle as the sun started to set on the mountains.

I sat and watched my companions as they kept busy, trying to fill the time. The anxiety in the camp was heavy. One thought pervaded every mind.

So far, their success and survival had been due to their ability to control the circumstances of their attack. Prior intelligence, tactical planning and outright luck had carried them so far.

In this attack, they would be totally committed in the center of the enemy's territory. There would be no diversions or tricks that would work if things started to go badly. The numbers would simply overwhelm them and all that would be left would be choosing how one died.

Frankly, it would be an outstanding success if they pulled it off with only one casualty. Thinking that they would get off completely scot-free would be foolhardy, and everyone was looking around, wondering who they might be seeing for the last time.

Joseph and Simeon picked their own spot by the fire when they weren't taking their turns on patrol. They spoke quietly, arguing at times, though not loudly enough for any of the rest of us to hear.

My guess would be that each of them was trying to convince the other to save himself if events turned sour. From the frustrated looks on both of their faces, I also guessed neither one was having any success.

The two were a matched set. While Simeon's ideals were more noticeable, Joseph's ideal of loyalty was just as absolute.

Chapter 22

I remember all the great moments, those times that are so powerful, all I can do is stand still and witness.

–Musings of the Historian

Getting into the castle was as easy as Yaltus said it would be. A crowd had formed at the gates long before a beefy Marauder guard came to let them into the castle proper. Inside, a line of Marauder captains waited to hear what each had to say.

The would-be informers would tell their story. If what they had to offer seemed to check out, they were waved to another man who sat at a rough table and doled out gold coins or sacks of some kind of food grain.

There was no particular order to the process and people pushed and shoved to get around each other. The desperation was clear in these people's faces. Most of them were women, though the men who were there seemed worst of all. I can't help but think that those were fathers with sick or starving children at home.

It has been said that a cobweb is as good as a steel cable if there is no strain upon it. Nowhere is that more clear than among the desperate.

Well-fed and with their families safe, I suspect any one of these people would have died rather than betray their fellow men. But when faced with the moans of the dying and the pain of loved ones, even the strongest morals falter.

Of course, for those whose morals were never more than cobwebs, even the slightest disruption is enough justification for them to feed their darker desires. It is no surprise that the first source of "information" usually comes from those carrying deep grudges.

The course of human history stands as proof that there is no ideal or motivation so pure that it cannot be turned to evil use. So it was with a delicious irony that we took advantage of this trend of treachery to accomplish something good.

We arrived individually and spent our time pushing and shoving with the rest of the crowd, letting ourselves be pushed back and forth by people trying to get closer or trying to get out.

Finally, Yaltus appeared around the corner of a nearby outbuilding and waved us over. Again, we went over one at a time, usually with some pretext.

In the end, however, nobody was paying us any attention; we could have all linked arms and skipped over to Yaltus and I don't think a single person would have noticed or cared.

"The fates smile on us, my noble lord." Yaltus whispered to Tibian. "Extra guards were pulled from their regular stations to help with the large crowd today. The door to the storage wing is completely unguarded.

"I heard that there will be a feast later. If we can get the poison into the Master's wine, he is sure to drink it tonight!"

He led us through the courtyard around to a gap between a tower and the outside wall. The effect was a curving hallway with towering walls on both sides. It came to an end when the wall closed with the tower, creating a pinched space where the two curved walls met. The effect was like the pointed end of a crescent moon. Before the two walls joined, there was a small wooden door set into the tower.

"Oh no! They've locked it!" Yaltus moaned as he came upon the door and tugged on the rough iron lock that was set on the hasp of the door. "We might need to call the whole thing off!"

Asher stepped forward and pushed Yaltus away from the door. He leaned down and pulled small steel picks from one of his pockets. He muttered curses at Yaltus and the steward backed away.

He leaned in and worked on the lock as the rest of us looked on over his shoulder. Finally, something inside the lock clicked and the hasp swung free. Asher tugged on the door to open it.

Nothing happened.

Joseph, being closest, leaned in and the two of them together strained against the door, but the heavy block might as well have been part of the stone for all it moved.

"Yaltus, is there another..." Tibian turned to ask his steward a question, but the words caught in his throat.

Ranks of Marauder warriors filled the passage behind us, twisting around the narrow passage beyond their sight. They were fully armored and their swords were drawn, though they were still far enough back so as not to be heard as they were sneaking up.

Yaltus was already walking towards them.

"Yaltus, get back here!" The king commanded. "What are you doing?"

"I am doing what I must, sire." The sniveling tone was

206

gone. Yaltus' voice held contempt for his former king as he turned to face him. "You're weak, and you've always been weak. A man needs to be smart and look after himself. That is what I'm doing.

"If I had turned you in alone, I would have been set for life. But now, I have got you, Gholost, and even the 'guerrilla band' that was causing so much trouble.

"I have handed the Master this whole country and the rewards will be beyond what even a king would enjoy.

"Frankly, in the long run, I think this nation will be better off under the command of a strong ruler, like the Master. Goodbye, my liege."

With that, Yaltus turned and walked through the Marauders, their ranks parting for him before settling back into their formation. Knowing that they would be facing Asher, the front ranks advanced at a slow creep, their formation shoulder to shoulder, swords out and long spears guarding them from the rear.

Asher spoke quickly to the rest of us, though he never took his eyes off of the advancing Marauder line.

"Look to where the walls meet. The hallway becomes thin enough that you can brace yourselves between the walls and climb to the top.

"When you make it to the top, go back the way we came about fifty paces. The river curves close to the wall and the water is deep enough that you'll survive if you jump. You can make it back to the woods from there."

"There isn't enough time," Tibian protested. "They would cut us down before even one of us made it to the top."

"You'll have enough time, but you must go now." Asher

commanded. Simeon and Joseph both understood what he intended in the same moment and Joseph started to protest.

"We're not going to..." Asher struck him across the face with the back of his hand.

"We don't have time for foolishness, boy! Move!"

As Asher turned back to the marching Marauders, his eyes caught mine for a fraction of a second and held. I nodded slightly and he smiled.

It wasn't the dark, sadistic smile that I had seen before. It was a warm smile that spoke of hope.

Then it was gone. Simeon had already grabbed Tibian and shoved him toward the meeting of the walls. The king started to climb, using all four limbs and even his head sometimes to work his way up, wedging himself into the stone crevice. Joseph was right behind him and then I was climbing, with Simeon right behind me.

The sounds of battle already echoed below us as we climbed, the Marauders must have rushed forward when they saw our possibility of escape. Tibian reached the top of the wall and turned to help the rest of us get on top of the wall.

"Move!" Simeon ordered, pushing all of us down the wall. From on top, we could see the river and where it bent close to the wall. I turned to watch Asher. Simeon and Joseph grabbed my arms to pull me along with them.

This simply would not do.

My purpose, my very reason for existence, was to witness great stories. Now I was being pulled away from one of the greatest final scenes I would ever see.

I knew that Simeon and Joseph would never agree to leave

me behind. They would stay behind and try to talk me out of it. There was only one thing left to do.

I drew myself up to my full height and dropped all pretense and disguise. I stood before them, not as a wanderer or vagabond, but as The Historian, with the wisdom and authority of a hundred kings burning in my eyes.

There is a sense of awe deep in our hearts when we look upon a newborn baby or an ancient man. It gives us the slightest glimpse of eternity. In someone like me, it is more than a glimpse. It was eternity that I let them see in me.

Joseph released my arm and took a step back. Simeon still held my arm, but confusion alternated with fear in his eyes as his mind tried to process something that didn't make sense standing before him.

"Leave." I spoke softly, but my tone was calculated to penetrate. I knew the tones and cadences of authority and I spoke like a king of legend. It had the desired effect as the two men stumbled away from me, running after their king. I watched long enough for the first one to leap from the wall into the river, then I turned back to the scene below.

I knew that I wouldn't be able to rejoin the group. It wouldn't be like it was before, not with what I had shown them. But there was no way I could miss this opportunity.

I would witness the death of Asher.

The scene below was pure carnage. Asher had his two hooks out and already had bodies around his feet. As he spun and slashed his way through his attackers, he was never off balance, even for a moment.

The Marauders, on the other hand, tripped over

themselves and over the bodies at their feet as they tried to reach him with sword and spear.

The tide turned when some of the Marauders managed to slip behind Asher into the space we had just left. Now they had him surrounded. The extra effort of fighting enemies on all sides took all he had to give. More Marauders made it around him.

Asher still hacked and slashed at anyone foolish enough to get close enough, but the Marauders were getting smarter. The swords were abandoned, most of their owners bleeding out on the ground.

Long spears surrounded Asher on all sides, stabbing and prodding. Whenever he managed to slip by the steel points to take down another warrior, the spot was filled instantly and the sharp circle of spearheads drew a little tighter.

It was absolutely amazing that any man could survive such a thing as long as Asher did. He was completely lost in the moment, dedicated body and soul to this last battle, the one he would carry with him to the other side.

At any given moment, three or four spears were jabbing at him. Without any armor, a single lapse in focus would mean death. Spear after spear missed or was pushed aside as Asher spun and dipped through the inverted porcupine of spears. As he dipped low, he would sweep feet out from under people, creating mayhem amid the ranks of warriors.

As he went high, he would block spears with one hand as his other hand threw knives that sought out weaknesses and chinks in the armor. The cries of pain blended together like a hellish choir, fitting music for the final scene of such a man.

There came a moment when Asher made a try at slipping

by again and a spear point from behind dug deep into the back of his thigh.

Asher stumbled.

With a roar, he threw himself into the Marauders where they were thinnest, right up against the wall. Two more Marauders fell, but Asher got another spear point in his shoulder in return.

The effort also bought him a better position as he fought his way to the wall and set himself against it, one side finally protected.

He dropped his hooks and dealt with the spears directly. He would grab onto them as they jabbed at him and pull hard. If the spearman got pulled with it, he was grabbed by Asher, his bones broken as the dark man used him as a temporary shield.

If the man had the sense to let go of his spear, Asher would spin the longer weapon and lash out at those within range.

More Marauders fell.

Asher was slowing. His wounds bled openly, and more had been added each time he extended himself to attack. A small pool was forming at his feet.

The end came when he got his hands on a spear and lashed out at a Marauder to his right. For the first and last time, Asher missed.

The spear missed the man and skipped off his armor. The Marauder's spear was more sure and drove through Asher's chest.

The rest of the Marauders were not foolish enough to wait and see if it would stop him. At this moment of ultimate weakness, the entire horde swept on top of him with spears and swords and I could see him no more.

Chapter 23

Hidden amongst the saddest stories is a strange truth:
Nothing can stop a man who is prepared to lose everything.
–Musings of the Historian

I could no longer be a participant in the story. The mystery of who I was would become the focus of their thoughts. While I felt a little sad at that, I wasn't sorry. It had been worth it.

It meant that now I would have to watch them as best I could without letting them know I was there. While I was very good at stealth, it's still hard to get close enough to hear conversation. A lot of the depth would be lost, not being able to hear the discussions.

The end couldn't be far off, though. The little band had lost nearly everything that could be considered an advantage. Their chances were small to begin with, and they had burned away like dry leaves in a forest fire with Yaltus' betrayal.

For all I knew, the story might already be over.

I went back to the camp in the forest, taking care to keep my distance. The trees weren't quite thick enough to give cover close in.

The three men moved stiffly as they gathered up materials from the camp. They rushed to leave the area while struggling to process what had happened to them.

The loss of Asher was devastating.

In many ways, lacking Yaltus' intelligence reports was just as bad. Though now they knew that Yaltus only fed them information to lead them up to one final trap.

I suddenly regretted not staying around the castle. I wish I could see Yaltus' reaction, or the Master's, for that matter, when it was found out that their perfect trap had only yielded up one target.

While the death of Hunger would no doubt be greatly celebrated among the Marauders, it would still seem like a loss when compared with what they thought they had.

It was no use looking back on stories lost, though. I focused back on the men as they finished their preparations. They had to know that soldiers would already be on their way to the camp. Yaltus knew where the camp was, and that meant the Marauders knew where the camp was.

When each of the men had a heavy pack on his back, Simeon struck out at a quick pace. It didn't take me long to recognize where they were going. They were headed to Simeon's camp, where he had taken Tibian when he thought he was rescuing Joseph.

Simeon led them through a couple backtracks and dead ends in case anyone tried to track them. Honestly, there had been enough patrols through the woods that any tracks would become confused with others within a mile or two.

I have met a couple of trackers capable of tracking them in those conditions, but they were few and far between. Nothing I had seen in this world led me to believe that there was anybody among the Marauders who could pull it off. If there were, all of us would have been caught long ago.

The scene back at the new camp was frustration, anger, and mourning. When the men talked, it was in argument. Simeon had planned his camp to give him a good line of sight, so I couldn't get close enough to hear what was said, but it was obvious that these men were hurt and confused.

I'm sure I was a topic of conversation a time or two, but the mystery of one unknown person would not hold ground against several known dangers.

From body language, it appeared that each man took a turn suggesting some course of action and the other two answered with vehement objections.

They had lost friends and they had lost hope. It was more than understandable that they took their frustrations out on one another.

There simply wasn't anyone else.

Somehow, the camp still functioned and they made it through setting up and a simple dinner, arguing the whole time. Joseph even shoved his brother during one heated exchange, though I couldn't guess what the cause would have been.

Simeon didn't reciprocate, and nothing came of it, but it showed the depth of despair that these men had reached.

All of them turned in early, before it even got dark. No guard was posted. At that moment, they were broken, too broken to care whether they got caught or not.

It made me sad to think that this was the end of the story. This small band wouldn't stick together long with the contention running so close to the surface, and they wouldn't survive long as individuals. The grand plan would simply fizzle away in the darkness, punctuated by a couple public executions.

I didn't regret the time spent, however. Asher's story alone was enough for my Historian soul. Some might say it was a sad one, as it ended in death, but all stories do.

I didn't feel the pull to start walking again, though that didn't mean much, it didn't always come when I expected it.

Movement attracted my eye and I realized that I had been sitting for hours watching the camp, lost in my own thoughts and musings about lost friends. The movement came from the camp and I realized that it was one of the men sneaking out.

Things hadn't gone so badly that it would require someone to sneak out, so this could only mean that one of the men meant to do something drastic.

I remembered Asher's words about how Joseph would want to be close enough to the situation to do something stupid for his brother. Of course, Simeon might be returning to his private war.

I cursed myself for not paying more attention to where each man had bedded down for the night. I must have been more distracted than I thought.

I followed the man through the night. He was heading back to the castle. On two occasions, he dropped to the ground and held still while torch-bearing patrols passed in the night, no doubt combing the area around the old camp.

Finally the man approached the edge of the city and settled into the abandoned house we had used when we set the trap for Joseph.

The whole time, I tried to sneak around enough to see his face, but the night was cloudy and there wasn't enough light to make him out.

Of our original party, only Asher and Yaltus were distinctive enough to make them out in the dark, the king and the brothers were too physically similar to recognize them in the dim light.

There was nothing for it but to sit and wait. From where I sat, I could see both exits from the house, and I could outwait anyone.

I expected him to move when it got light, perhaps in some sort of disguise, but the day wore on with no sign of my mysterious companion. It was late afternoon when something finally caught my attention. It wasn't from the house, it was from the castle.

Yaltus had crossed over the castle bridge. He was dressed in fine velvet robes. Heavy gold chains clinked around his neck and bright gems adorned rings on every finger.

Unlike the crouching, sniveling servant I had known, Yaltus now walked fully upright, his head held high with all the pride of a servant become master.

With my attention diverted, I barely looked back in time to see King Tibian striding toward his steward. There was no disguise, though the run through the woods and the rough sleep of the night before had given him the lean, haggard look of a lone wolf.

Yaltus recognized him a moment too late. His eyes grew as large as saucers and he opened his mouth to scream as Tibian closed on him and ran him through with his father's sword.

The ex-steward clawed at the sword for a long moment before slouching to the ground like a deflated balloon. Even the

216

guards who stood by the castle were momentarily stunned as they watched Tibian calmly wipe the blood from Stephan's sword with Yaltus' luxurious robe.

The guards were closing on him when Tibian raised his sword and shouted his demand.

"I challenge the Master!" The guards paused at this, looking at one another, trying to decide what to do. The king took advantage of the moment.

"I am King Tibian and I say that the Master is a weakling and a coward! Let him face me as a man, rather than send his traitors!"

More guards flowed out of the castle, but they moved to encircle the king, not to capture him. Once they were certain he wasn't escaping, they didn't seem to be in much of a hurry to take him down.

Something he had said excited either their curiosity or blood lust. They seemed more than happy to pass his message up the line.

Through the castle gates, I could see messengers at a dead sprint toward the castle. The Master would know of the king's challenge before Yaltus was cold.

Tibian nodded approvingly and started walking to the market square. His circle of Marauder guards moved with him, like an honor guard before a duel.

The market was full, but everyone scattered in front of this circle of Marauder blades. No one left, though; all eyes were on their king. Tibian stood at the center of the circle, a look of absolute peace on his face. It was the look of a man committed to his course.

A thought occurred to me and I searched the faces of the gathered throng. Sure enough, I picked out the brothers standing on the outskirts, craning their necks to see over the crowd. Simeon's expression was grim, Joseph's was absolutely panicked.

Knowing that their attention was riveted on the king, I left my spot and circled around the market to stand behind the two of them.

Simeon held a scrap of paper in his hand. His fist was closed so tightly that white showed on every knuckle. It didn't take much thought to realize what had happened. The king had left a note for his general, instructions for his part in this new insane plan.

A roar of approval rumbled from the castle. The Master had made his appearance. Nothing was changing with the brothers, so I wove my way through the crowd to get a better look. By the time I made it to the front of the mass of spectators, the Master was breaking through as well.

I swallowed hard. I knew in that moment that the king didn't stand a chance. The Master was a behemoth of a man, seven feet tall if he was an inch.

Thick coiling pads of muscle covered the man like a sculpture made flesh. Calluses on his hands spoke of endless training with the sword, and scars dotting his body told of pain endured and battles won. He stood in his element like a god of war.

Ten skilled soldiers, working together with a prearranged plan might have brought this man down, but no fewer than that. I realized now that Yaltus had been being diplomatic when he said that the Master might have been Asher's match.

218

Although I had personally witnessed how lethal Asher could be, this was another level entirely. I doubted that Asher could have matched the Master, even in his prime.

Furthermore, the harsh truth was that, for all his brutality, Asher had already grown old, his wars behind him. He would have fallen had he faced the Master in one on one combat, as the king now proposed to do.

The guards surrounding Tibian fell away. I understood why they hadn't bothered to take him themselves. This would be a much more entertaining spectacle for them.

Tibian brought up his sword, Stephan's sword, and roared his defiance again.

"I challenge you! I am not afraid of you! You are weak! And I, I am king!"

The smile on the Master's face was a dreadful thing. A scar across his lips pulled the smile into a lopsided leer. Unevenness notwithstanding, the sheer joy in the smile was unnerving.

He wouldn't just kill Tibian, he would chop him into pieces in front of all his people. It would be a show of strength his people would remember forever.

The sword he drew looked ridiculous in his massive hands. I had expected something monstrous, something to match the man. Instead the sword looked like a small stick in comparison.

It took me a moment to realize the intentional nature of his choice. It was a sword exactly like Tibian's. He would leave no doubt as to the purity of his victory. It was clear to every mind in that market.

No advantage would be taken, none was needed.

I wish I could tell a tale of great combat, a clash between rulers, but Tibian was lost before it began.

The battle was short.

Tibian fell into the stance Asher had taught him and raised his sword to meet the Master's attack. The Master was no hulking brute, he moved light on his feet and was on the king in the blink of an eye.

The first couple swings of his sword were fast and heavy. They hit only air as Tibian danced away, always keeping in his stance.

The Master laughed as he pursued Tibian across the square. Tibian barely made it clear of his opponent's swings as he dodged backward. Only once did he try to block the other man's sword with his own and he almost lost his sword for his efforts.

Finally the Master feinted, shuffling forward as if to swing again. The king fell for it and started his dodge back. The Master shot forward, switching feet and lunging in a long stab to where Tibian had to land.

The maneuver was perfect and Tibian had nowhere to go, his feet barely landing as the other man's sword slid into his torso.

Tibian's hand flashed to the blade as it pushed through him and did a strange thing...

He pulled.

The motion tugged on the Master, already fully extended in his lunge. He lost his balance for just a moment, a stutter step to regain his center.

Tibian, still in his stance with the Master's sword buried deep in his body, flashed out with his own sword. The Master's reach was such that Tibian could not have dealt a mortal blow. Instead, his blade slashed at the Master's extended sword arm, severing it above the wrist.

The Master roared and followed up with a massive kick that sent the king tumbling, the sword still in his chest. The move was unnecessary, Tibian was already collapsing under his own weight when the kick landed. He stayed where he fell in a lump. He lifted his head and smiled at the Master, blood in his teeth.

"Weak." He whispered. Fear flashed across the Master's face as he glanced down to the blood flowing from his severed arm and he held it tight under his other arm to cut off the flow.

He started to move toward the king. The ultimate warrior, he would finish the battle by stomping the life out of Tibian.

A flurry of cloaks rushed from the crowd and men with swords surrounded the king. Their leader looked back to where the king sat in the dirt.

"Do you know where Asher is? We've been trying to find him. Speak quickly, your time is short."

"He is dead. Who are you?" Tibian's voice was already weak and rasping as his ribs tried to work around the wedge of steel.

In answer, the man pulled down the shoulder of his tunic, revealing a scar that ran along his shoulder, identical to the one Asher had given Tibian.

"Asher's men." Tibian nodded, understanding. The Master had paused in the face of this new threat. If he had a sword in his hand, he might have attacked the older soldiers anyway, but his wound made it suicide without one. The leader of the soldiers raised his sword to counterattack.

"NO!" The king's command ripped from his throat like a death scream and the soldier stopped and backed up to his line, obeying the command. "Let him leave."

As if following the same command, the Master stumbled from the yard, bellowing at his followers for help.

The effect on the Marauders of seeing their leader crippled was more than anyone could have hoped. They milled and fidgeted. Only a few loyal warriors followed the Master, forming an armed circle to guard his retreat, similar to the one surrounding the king.

I noticed a lot of Marauders leave the crowd. Their armor was slightly different from one another and from the Master's. These were men from different tribes.

They were going back to their own tribal leaders to report what had happened. Their loyalty to their own tribe overrode any concern for the king or the Master.

The confusion and the protection of Asher's old squad allowed Simeon and Joseph to slip in and gather up the king, now laying limp on the ground.

The soldiers led them to the outskirts of town, near to the inn where I had first entered the town so many months ago. It looked like my story would get a little symmetry after all.

Chapter 24

There is wisdom out there that can't be relayed in musings or sage advice. Like the complexity of life itself, it simply won't condense. It can only be shown in its entirety. It takes a story.

-Musings of the Historian

When it was clear which house they were going to, I went ahead, determined not to be left out of the loop again. I decided the best place was on the roof.

The fire wasn't lit now that the weather was warm, and the chimney gave me a broad listening ear to what was happening in the house. All I had was dialogue, but it was enough.

"Who are you?" The leader of the soldiers spoke.

"I am Simeon, son of Ander, general to the king." He spoke bravely enough, but his voice was choked with emotion. "This is my brother, Joseph. Who are you?"

"We are Asher's men. He trained us and kept us safe during the war. He disappeared after the incident with your father. We heard later he was living in the slums, but we never managed to find him.

"You don't find Asher unless he wants to be found. When we heard about him fighting the Marauders, we thought he might finally want our help. I gathered the others and we've been trying to find him for weeks. It sounds like we are too late."

"I'm afraid you're right, we were betrayed last night and Asher fell giving us the time to get away."

"How many were there?"

"A whole army, and ready for him."

"I am sorry to hear it. Did any of you witness his final moments?"

"I did not." Simeon's voice was heavy with sorrow. "One of our companions stayed behind to watch, but we haven't seen him either."

"What companion? Another warrior? I would dearly love to speak with him if he was there. All of my men would give much to hear of Asher's last struggle."

"Not a warrior, some sort of storyteller. I don't believe we will see him again if he doesn't wish it, though. He was more than what he seemed, of that I'm certain."

"That is a shame." The old soldier's words carried all the admiration and regret he carried for Asher. He changed the subject.

"So this is Stephan's son? I thought he would be softer, what with all that castle living. That fight was something amazing. Those stances, it was like seeing a young Asher out there on the field."

"He was softer," Joseph chimed in. "At least on the outside. Once things got bad, though, he showed that he was made of tougher stuff. Do you think he'll live?"

"I doubt it." I could almost hear the shrug in the older man's voice. "He's lost blood and he'll lose a lot more when we take that sword out. The shock is sparing him a lot of the pain right now, but when that wears off, it will likely be too much for his system.

"It's an awful waste, I see now what a great king he would have been. Though I can't say he showed a lot of sense, picking a fight he couldn't win."

"He never intended to win." Simeon offered and I heard a crinkle of paper, likely the note Tibian had left behind changing hands. Long moments of silence dragged on as the soldier read the letter and digested its meaning. He whistled softly in amazement.

"That's an awful long shot. Do you really think they'll break apart like that?"

"It was our best plan, but I thought it hopeless once we lost Asher."

"And this is Joseph, you said?"

"What?" Joseph's tone was shocked. I guessed he hadn't read the letter. "What does it say about me?"

"He named you his heir," Simeon explained softly, "To become king when he fell."

"What?!" Joseph sounded outraged. "Why would he do a thing like that? I don't want to be king!"

"I suspect that is why you'd make a good one." Simeon observed. "Still, let's hope it doesn't come to that. We still have a good king right here, as long as he keeps breathing."

The only sounds after that were men shuffling around, caring for the king. At one juncture, there was a rough, high-pitched gurgle. It must have been when they pulled the sword out. A man that close to death can't always manage a scream.

There was nothing to do, so I went for a walk.

It was a long walk.

I followed sounds of violence and at times I found people fighting small bands of Marauders, with varying degrees of success.

In a couple instances, I found Marauders fighting other Marauders. They weren't pitched battles, more like duels or drunken brawls, but it showed the breakdown of order that was already running through the Marauders like a plague.

My walk took longer than I had planned and weeks passed as I wandered from one skirmish to another. The plan wasn't going exactly as Simeon had hoped, but it was still effective.

Marauders were fighting Marauders. I often caught glimpses of Simeon around these battles, though I never let him see me.

When one tribe would win out over another, Simeon would lead his forces in an attack on the worn-out soldiers, striking from ambush just as they thought their battle was over.

As his victories grew, so did his armies. He was smart enough not to keep them all together. I recognized faces in the various bands that would attack Marauders when they were too weak to resist or too strong to be challenged by others.

Simeon had used Asher's old death squad to good effect. Each seasoned soldier was now a captain of a resistance band, lending their experience and the legend of their teacher to the men they led.

Things didn't always go well. There were outlying towns that were completely ravaged when one tribe of Marauders decided to leave and take everything they could on their way out.

Still, these losses were rare enough. The kingdom was

winning the war, and they didn't even fight that many battles.

Simeon soon learned which armor belonged to which tribe and would dress up his own raiders in enemy armor to breed anger among the tribes as they thought old allies were stealing their supplies.

I finally made my way back to the little house where I had last seen Tibian. No lights burned and the place was abandoned. There was no way to tell whether the king had survived or not.

It took another two weeks before the Marauders grew weak enough that the new Land Guard was able to take the castle.

I was out of position when it happened,. There had been a battle between tribes and I had been sitting on the sidelines to watch.

It wasn't until after the battle that I heard that General Simeon had used the diversion to make a strike at the castle. I rushed back as fast as I could.

News had traveled fast and the scene was still chaos as citizens and soldiers wove in and out of the castle gate freely.

The Land Guard was gone, probably off making sure the defeated tribe, with the Master at its head, didn't double back for revenge.

It was an easy thing for me to slip in unnoticed. My sense of unease grew as I searched from room to room, checking every bed for the king. I knew it was a long shot, but I still allowed myself to hope.

When I had searched every room, finding no one, I decided it was probably time to move on. I took my path out of the castle by way of the throne room, which had no windows and was almost completely dark.

"Storyteller."

As I have mentioned before, it isn't easy to surprise a Historian, but I jumped like I'd been scalded and spun to see Tibian, sitting up in the throne, his chest a mess of bandages.

"How did you recognize me? Is there a light around here?"

Tibian reached out a hand and pulled an overturned pot off of a lantern that was already burning. Light flooded the room. Tibian smiled at me.

"I didn't recognize you. Simeon told me you would come back here. He also told me what he saw on top of that wall."

"What did he say he saw?"

"He said he didn't know, but that you were more than some wanderer. He said he didn't think you could leave without knowing the end of the story, any more than you could leave Asher at the end."

"So how did you know I would show up here today?"

"I didn't. I've been waiting every day since I woke up. Really, sitting in the dark isn't so bad when you have nothing else to do."

"How long has it been since you woke up?"

"Only a few days, actually. Mendar says it's amazing I woke up at all."

"Is Mendar the name of Asher's soldier, the one who leads the others?"

"That's right. He's now second-in-command. He has been of great help implementing Simeon's strategy."

"How is that going?"

"Better than I could have hoped. The Master is still in

control of his own tribe and one other, but they have lost the castle, as you can see. Even one handed, he is a force to be reckoned with.

"We were lucky to take the castle back, we caught them when their armies were out fighting another tribe. Now that we command its walls, though, they won't be able to take it back from us. We won't make the same mistake they did in underestimating their enemy."

"What about the rest of the tribes?"

"The weaker tribes saw themselves about to be caught between a hammer and an anvil and almost all of them have already gone back to their own lands.

"There were a couple that went rogue and tried to carve out their own pieces, but territory disputes between them and the Master have left them weak enough that our own soldiers were enough to drive them off."

"I've got to say, I'm amazed it has gone so smoothly."

"I am being upbeat about it. The war goes well, but we have lost plenty of battles. We lost an entire squad yesterday when they were pinned down on a raid.

"The biggest element has been the loyalty to tribe that Asher told us about. It seems that a lot of these tribes were only here as long as it seemed like a sure thing. Leaving their own lands defenseless has put quite a strain on them.

"Simeon's guerrilla war and the crippling of the Master put enough doubt into their minds that most were eager to get back to their own homes, or to the homes of their rivals, if you get my meaning.

"Mendar says that even the big tribes still fighting here

will likely rush to return when they hear about their own homelands being attacked."

"Are you sure that their homelands will be attacked?"

"Mendar says that if their rivals back home don't get to it, he and his boys will see to it personally."

The door behind me burst open and Joseph and Simeon rushed into the room, swords drawn. When they saw me, they lowered their swords, though they didn't sheath them.

"We saw the light under the door." Joseph offered. "We came as fast as we could. We worried it would be someone else. It looks like you were right, Simeon."

Simeon's eyes were locked on me, as if I might suddenly vanish from his sight if he blinked.

"Who are you? What is your name?" The story had truly come full circle, and we were right back to the beginning.

"I don't have one."

This time, he nodded, his skepticism gone.

"Will you stay with us?" This question came from behind me, from Tibian.

"No, this story is done. I need to be getting on to the next one."

"Why did you come back?" Joseph asked.

"I had a question to ask Tibian. If he had died, this would have been my last stop."

"What is your question, Storyteller? I will answer it if I can."

"Why did you fight the Master, knowing that you would almost certainly die?"

King Tibian frowned as he thought of an appropriate

answer. His face suddenly brightened as he looked up at me and smiled.

"My carving was in the fire."

I nodded, smiling back. I walked over and put my hand on his head, as if in blessing.

"You'll be a fine king, Tibian."

I turned to leave and Simeon and Joseph moved to block my way.

"We still have questions for you, though."

"I still have questions for myself." I shrugged and moved past them to the door.

"Wait!" The call came from Simeon and I turned slightly. "You promised to judge me! You yourself say the story is over. Judge me now for my part in it, I beg you."

It was the most emotion I had ever seen from Simeon, and I remembered the need that was in his voice the first time he had made his request.

I searched for the words that would tell him what he wanted to know. In the end, there was only one answer. I put my hand on his shoulder and leaned in to whisper in his ear.

"Your father would be proud of you."

I pulled back to see the tears welling in his eyes as he nodded, not trusting himself to speak. I stepped forward impulsively and hugged Joseph, the almost-king.

Goodbyes done, I left the castle, that city, and that land. I felt the compulsion to see new land, but I didn't need it to drive me.

This was a wonderful story, the kind that come around but rarely. This was the sort of story that made you proud to be a part of it, a story that made you believe in people again, and I am glad I got to share it with you. After all…

This was a story about you.

About the Author

Lance Conrad lives in Utah, surrounded by loving and supportive family who are endlessly patient with his many eccentricities. His passion for writing comes from the belief that there are great lessons to be learned as we struggle with our favorite characters in fiction. He spends his time reading, writing, building lasers, and searching out new additions to his impressive collection of gourmet vinegars.

For more from the author, read his blog at:

thehistoriantales.blogspot.com

What is possible with an Historian in command?

The Historian finds himself in a deal with the devil as he must make himself part of the story in exchange for information about his own past. In fires of magic, love, and loyalty, the Historian must make a story his own.

Look for The Price of Loyalty, coming out in print in 2014 from Dawn Star Press

www.dawnstarpress.com

For updates, follow author Lance Conrad on Twitter: @LanceConradlit